Love's Rescue

By Linda Shenton Matchett

Love's Rescue

By Linda Shenton Matchett

ISBN-13: 978-0-9985265-4-6

Published by Shortwave Press

To

Valerie Massey Goree and Marcia Lahti

For your friendship and support

Paris, August 1944

Chapter One

Rolande Bisset ducked her head and pulled the brim of her starched cotton sunhat lower over her face, not so much to block the sun's glare, but to avoid the merchants' ogling and shoppers' sneers. She hurried past the darkened shops, most no longer operating since the Germans arrived four years ago. Would she ever smell freshly-baked croissants or peruse a succulent collection of vegetables again?

A scorching breeze sent her hat's veil dancing. Perspiration trickled between her shoulder blades and threatened to ruin her cobalt-blue silk suit. Her pumps had seen better days, but thanks to leather rationing, a new pair was not in the offing. The Occupiers needed the material for their boots.

Intent upon reaching her destination, Rolande failed to see a rotund woman approaching. They collided, and the woman's elaborate *chapeau* slid from her upswept hair and poked Rolande in the face before landing on the pavement.

"I beg your pardon, madam." Rolande bent to retrieve the confection of flowers, birds, and ribbons.

The woman narrowed her eyes. "Watch where you're going, *collaborateur*." She snatched the millinery masterpiece from Rolande's grasp and drew her skirts close. Looking down her nose, she plunked the hat on her head and marched down the sidewalk.

Heat suffused Rolande's face, and it had nothing to do with the day's temperature. Unbidden tears sprang to her eyes. She blinked them away and stiffened her spine. She couldn't let anyone see how the women's words sliced her heart and her conscience.

No longer hungry, she continued down the avenue past Aux Cerises Café where the outdoor tables were filled with German soldiers. One of the men whistled and smirked, his Aryan features marred by a long scar that ran from his eye to his jaw. Her stomach clenched, and nausea threatened.

Pigs. Men were all pigs.

She continued along the avenue until she came to the tiny market her older brother owned. He never acknowledged her presence in the shop, but neither did he forbid her to enter. His wife typically looked at her with a mixture of pity and contempt.

The brass bell jangled above her head as she pushed open the door and stepped inside. Vacant shelves greeted her, and she sighed. Most patrons were smart enough to come first thing in the morning for the best selection, but she had been *entertaining.*

Little did he realize, *Standartenführer* Wilhelm Wagner was one of her most reliable sources for information. Tipsy when he arrived; before he left at the end of the evening, he was deep in his cups. With minimal prodding, he'd told her about the anticipated invasion by the Allied troops.

Sure, the rumor had been circulating among civilians, but to hear it from a military man made the possibility plausible.

Liberation, at last.

"I set this aside for you."

Rolande's head whipped around.

Her sister-in-law, Louise, stood behind her, a brown-paper package in her hands. She looked toward the door then shoved the parcel into Rolande's arms. "You are later than usual, and I was concerned there'd be no food remaining. There are a few potatoes and carrots in the bin, but nothing else."

"You're very kind."

"It's nothing. Now, hurry before Henri returns."

"*Je vous remercie.* Why are you doing this?"

Louise waved her hand and frowned. "There is no time. He is due any moment. Give me your ration book."

Rolande handed her the book. Her sister-in-law tore out the required stamps, then pushed the pamphlet back into Rolande's hand.

"How much do I owe you?"

"Nothing. We are *famille*, no matter how Henri acts."

For the second time that morning, Rolande's eyes filled with tears. She was getting soft. That would have to change for her to survive the Occupation. Dipping her head, she tucked the package into her canvas bag then threaded her way through the shop to the front door where she came face-to-face with Henri.

Visage dark, he scowled. "Did anyone see you come here?"

"The whole world, Henri. It is a public street. Would you like me to wear a disguise in the future? Perhaps sunglasses and a wig."

"*Non.* What I would like is for you to find somewhere else to purchase your food."

Louise gasped. "Henri. She is your sister."

His lips compressed into a thin line, and he crossed his arms. "She is dead to me."

Rolande drew back as if he'd slapped her. He'd always been condescending, but to declare her dead…the words cut through her.

"Fine. I will not bother you again." She pushed past him into the stifling heat. Where would she find food? Two other shops in town had already refused to serve her.

Oblivious to the deprivation and sadness in Paris, birds chirped and flitted in the branches above Rolande's head in the *Jardin de Champs Élysées.* She sat on the scarred wooden bench listening to the water pour over the Fontaine du Cirque. Listless yellow and purple blooms nodded at her from the fountain's base. At least with the Germans' love of art, they hadn't destroyed the nearly three-hundred-year-old park.

Rolande closed her eyes. *Are You there, God? Do you exist like the priest in the café said? If You are real, You have no reason to answer me, an unworthy woman of ill repute, but why did You allow this terrible war? Are the rumors accurate that the Allies are on their way?*

If only it was true. Would they take her with them to a land of freedom and democracy where she could start a new life? Tears coursed down her cheeks. She was fooling herself to think she had skills that would enable her to get a real job to support herself. No country would let her across their borders.

Footsteps sounded behind her then the bench groaned in protest as someone sat next to her. She peeked through slitted eyelids at a large body squeezed into a German SS uniform. Swallowing a curse, she forced a smile and opened her eyes. "Wilhelm, I would ask how you found me, but your men are everywhere."

Wilhelm ran his forefinger along her jawline. His smile transformed his boyish face into a rapacious demeanor. "*Ja,* we patrol in order to keep you safe. What are you doing here in the middle of the day?"

"I was shopping, and it didn't go…well. My brother has forbidden me to frequent his market any longer. I came to consider my options." Despite the heat, her hands were chilled and stiff. She rubbed them together before sliding them into the folds of her skirt. "I only have a few tins put by."

"You should have come to me. As your special friend, I can ensure that you are provided for. You know that." He drew lazy circles on her shoulder.

She stifled a shudder. "You have been most generous, but I hesitated to bother you with something so petty."

"Silly *Liebchen,* I wouldn't let my beautiful *Schmetterling* waste away." He puffed out his chest. "It is my duty to ensure you and your countrymen are taken care of. Life is better now that we have arrived. Surely, you see that."

"You're right. I should have asked you."

He leaned toward her, a wolfish gleam in his eyes. "Perhaps I should come to you later. I will bring provisions, and you can prepare a delicious meal, compliments of the Third Reich. Then we can enjoy each other's company. *Ja?*"

Bile rose in Rolande's throat. His sweaty bulk combined with his arrogance disgusted her. There was nothing about him she enjoyed, but perhaps he had news. If she got him drunk enough, he'd share what he knew, then fall asleep before any physical contact was required.

"I would be happy to entertain you, Wilhelm, and I will wear your favorite dress. Be sure to bring wine. What I have is not fit for someone of your importance. Shall we say eight o'clock?"

"Why so late?" He frowned. "Will you be seeing others?"

"I have more errands to run, but yes, I will have visitors. You said it is helpful to your cause if I am able to ferret out information." Hopefully, he would never know how much of what she passed along was contrived in her own mind. She patted his cheek then drew back her hand. "I'm doing my part for the war effort."

He grabbed her wrist and held it in an iron grip. "As long as that is all you are doing."

It was useless to struggle when he became possessive, bullying her like he did everyone else, and it was dangerous to taunt him, but she couldn't resist a dig. "These men mean nothing to me. Besides, the war will be over soon, Wilhelm. The Americans will come, and you will return to Germany, your wife, and your son. I will be a distant memory that brings an occasional smile to your lips."

His face darkened. "What do you know of the *Amerikaners*?"

"Only what I hear in the streets; that they landed on the Normandy beaches and are headed this way. I am not looking forward to a clash on Parisian streets."

"They will not make it to Paris. We will stop them. They are not strong like us."

Rolande turned her gaze toward the sky. *Dear God, don't let that be so.*

Would the priest's unseen God hear her?

Chapter Two

Clanking metal, noxious fumes, and the murmur of a hundred conversations filtered through the tent wall from the American base camp located about twenty miles from Paris as First Lieutenant Simon Harlow rummaged through his kit for a pen. He hadn't written home in two weeks, and his parents would worry that he was dead.

His missives had begun to sound like elementary school projects. "Dear Mom, how are you? I am fine. The food here leaves much to be desired." But there was so little he could share. The censors would remove any references to locations, incidents, or any other perceived confidential information. What could he write now that a battle was on the horizon?

"Aha. There you are." His fingers grasped the pencil lodged between his canteen and a pair of socks. He pulled out the implement, sat on the ground, and leaned against the center pole in the M1934 Pyramidal tent, a large canvas contraption that slept eight men like spokes in a wheel.

The tent was vacant for the moment, and Simon reveled in the solitude. Off duty for the next two hours, he propped his notepad on his thigh, tapping his chin with the pen. What to say?

His stomach rumbled, and he began to write.

"Dear Mom, I received your latest letter and the accompanying cookies. Unfortunately, they were little more than crumbs when they arrived, but the boys and I enjoyed the bits of sweetness nonetheless. Please send more at your earliest convenience. We continue to wait while the senior officers to figure out what to do to get the best of ol' Jerry. You'd be proud of me learning to do my own wash. Officers don't normally do that sort of chore, but I needed to handle an issue with one of the men, and the best way to do it seemed to be elbowing up next to him in the laundry tent. He was surprised I was game to roll up my sleeves and do grunt work, so he was willing to hear what I had to say. Now, I'll make someone a good husband one of these days."

The tent flap opened, and First Lieutenant Eddie Dryden strode across the packed dirt floor. "Hey there, buddy, what are you doing hanging around in this stifling tent? At least outside, there's a breeze." He pulled a handkerchief from his pocket and mopped the sweat from his face. "Being the dutiful son, are you?"

"Yes, and it wouldn't hurt you to do the same. You've got to repair your relationship with your parents. What if you don't make it?"

Eddie snorted a laugh. "Then you'll do the right thing and tell them how very much I regretted not making up with them, or some other drivel that allows them to feel better." He scowled. "They are elitist and old-fashioned. To forbid me to enlist simply because I'm part of some rich, high-society family is ridiculous. We all have to do our part, especially the gentry. Your parents didn't try to purchase your way out. Life is going to change for that generation after the war, you know. Classes will be a thing of the past. Freedom is what we're fighting for, isn't it?"

Simon laid the letter on the ground and ran a finger around the collar that threatened to choke him. Three years in the army, and his body still seemed to reject the cotton and wool uniform. Three years since he'd worn hand-tailored suits and silk ties imported from Savile Row. Was he as much a highbrow as Eddie's parents?

He picked up the paper and climbed to his feet. Tucking the half-finished letter into his rucksack, Simon blew out a deep breath. "Sometimes I'm not sure what we're fighting for."

"Keep your voice down. Do you want Major Fremont to hear? The last time he overheard one of the boys say something like that, the poor guy was demoted and stuck with kitchen duty for a month."

"Funny you should say that. I just told Mom that I'd learned how to wash my own clothes." He pulled his damp shirt away from his chest. "And if this heat doesn't break, these shirts are going to need cleaning more than once a day."

Eddie dropped onto one of the canvas stools and waved a stained, wrinkled envelope. "Mail call." He slid a finger under the flap and withdrew a folded sheaf of paper. Holding it close to his nose, he inhaled deeply. "Lavender. That's my girl." He propped himself against the wall of the tent and began to read. The planes of his face relaxed, and a smile curved his lips. He rubbed the edge of the paper as if stroking the writer's hand.

With a frown, Simon circled the post, his soles kicking up dust.

A chuckle sounded behind him. "You're like a caged lion. Sit down and finish the letter to your parents. If we're to shove off soon like we think, you may not have another opportunity to write."

Simon snatched his knapsack from the ground with a growl. "What can I say that hasn't already been said?"

"It's not what you write that's important. It's that you write. I may not get along with Mom and Dad, but I know they love and miss me. The same goes for your parents. They want to know you are safe and sound." He slid the envelope into his breast pocket. "Too bad you're not walking out with some sweet gal. That might improve your mood."

"That's not going to happen any time soon."

"What? Your mood or the girl?"

"Probably both." Simon rubbed his forehead. "Do you think I'm too fussy? Even Jenkins has someone, and he seems a bit shifty to me, always skulking around, drinking every chance he gets, and trying to get out of drills and such."

"You have a right not to settle on anyone, but I think your parents must be ready for you to get serious about someone. After all, you're twenty-eight years old."

"A lifetime is too long to be paired with a poor match." Simon shrugged. "Perhaps God isn't finished preparing the poor gal to be able to handle a guy like me."

Eddie laughed. "Now, that's more like it. She'd have to be truly special to want to live out her days with you. You're handsome, wealthy, and even charming on your better days. Who could love a man like that?"

Simon grabbed a pillow from a nearby cot and tossed it at Eddie. The cushion sailed past his head and landed on the ground with a thud.

"Seriously, Simon, you've been a first-class chum, and God does have a girl out there for you. Have you prayed about it?"

"No. It seems uppity to put in an order for a wife, don't you think? What would I say? Can you please send me a dark-haired, willowy brunette with a penchant for cooking, cleaning, and children?"

"You're talking nonsense. 'Tis better to ask for a sweet Christian girl, full of integrity and faith."

Simon's face warmed. "You're right. Can I at least ask that she comes from a good family? That way, Mom and Dad will be happy too."

"There are lots of French girls who will be plenty grateful after we liberate Paris. Perhaps one of them will catch your eye."

"Doubtful. You've heard the stories. They're all collaborators. Giving Hitler's men whatever they want, and billeting them. No, I definitely won't be looking for a wife in Paris."

"Be careful, Simon. You've not walked in their shoes. If you had to choose between death for you and your family and playing along with the enemy, what would you do?"

"When did you get to be so wise?"

"I—"

A bugle screeched outside, and feet stampeded past the tent. A deep voice shouted, "Fall in; fall in!"

Eddie leapt to his feet. "Sounds like Paris might be sooner rather than later."

Simon's gaze whipped to the open tent flap then back at Eddie, eyes wide. His heart pounded, and sweat broke out on his palms. *Dear God, keep the boys and me safe this day. And if it's not too much trouble, could You allow me to live and find a sweet Christian girl to marry?*

Chapter Three

Hours after curfew, Rolande crept along the west bank of the
Seine. Darkness enveloped the city, but she knew the magnificent Eiffel
Tower stood tall and proud ahead of her. Breathless, her heart pounded. If
she was caught, the penalty would be harsh.

A scuffle sounded next to her, and she froze. A large rat kicked up
leaves, then scurried into the bushes. Enraged chatter split the air. She
shuddered. There was more than one of the filthy rodents, probably
several. Many of the disgusting creatures had taken up residence in Paris's
parks. Rolande shivered and continued to walk beside the brooding river,
silent and motionless as if it too didn't wish to be seen.

She patted her head to ensure the forbidden beret still remained on
her hair. A violation of one of the many mandates put in place after the
Germans arrived, but the woolen cap was necessary tonight to identify
herself to her contact. They would converse in French, her favorite law to
break.

Clouds scudded across the sky and blocked the waning moon,
making visibility even more difficult. No matter. As a Parisian, she could
walk the *boulevards* blindfolded and still find her way. Something the
Occupiers hadn't counted on when they ordered blackouts.

Dear God, I am not worthy of Your notice, but I would like to believe You exist and are watching over me. If You are there, please keep me safe, so I can pass necessary information to la Résistance. They need this to thwart the Occupiers' plans.

Despite the sun's disappearance, heat still shrouded the city's inhabitants. Perspiration formed under her arms and along her hairline. As she moved, moisture trickled down her spine, dampening her blouse.

Moments later she arrived at the rendezvous point. Rubbing her hands together, she ducked behind a gnarled tree. She strained to peer into the night. No one seemed to be here. Had her contact been unable to get away to meet her? Or worse, been caught?

Her shoulders knotted at the thought. If the person had been arrested, she could be in danger, too. Torture sometimes caused even the most stalwart person to crack. That was why *la Résistance* insisted on the use of aliases. Unknown information couldn't be given away.

The clouds parted, and moonlight filtered between the branches. A man's form appeared from behind a large shrub. He emitted a cricket-like chirp, and she mimicked the call. Slipping from her hiding place, she approached the man.

"The cock crows at midnight." Rolande's whispered words broke the silence.

"*Non.* Only at dawn." The man's sonorous voice rumbled in the darkness.

"*Bien.*" Rolande licked her dry lips. Was the intelligence obtained from two tipsy *Hauptsturmführers* accurate or did they know about her activities in *la Résistance*? Was she being set up?

"Hurry up. I haven't got all night."

"Of course. My apologies." She took a deep breath. "The *Wehrmacht* are deploying their men in two locations in anticipation of the Allies advance toward Paris." In clipped sentences and with several glances over her shoulder, she outlined the plans complete with locations, troop numbers, and movements that had tumbled unheeded from the lips of the men she'd plied with wine. Would the information prevent more deaths or escalate the carnage? She trembled as she finished talking.

"Is that everything?"

"*Oui.* Both men were anxious to impress me with their knowledge."

"And you have told no one else?"

"Why would I do that?" Rolande's voice broke.

"Because information is worth money, and women such as yourself want money and the lifestyle it brings." Scorn dripped from his words.

Her face heated, and she was glad for the cover of night. She straightened her spine. "And what would you know about women like me? Bah. You men are all alike, thinking you understand women, our needs, our wants. You know nothing. We women are keeping this country afloat."

She turned, and he grabbed her arm in a vicelike grip. He leaned close to her ear. "You keep thinking that, Rolande."

At the sound of her name, she gasped. Tears stung her eyes. Was this the end?

He released her, a harsh laugh thundering in his chest. "Now, go, and make sure you are not caught, or you'll wish you were never born."

"That is already my wish." She stalked away and hoped her quivering legs would hold her until she was out of sight. His footsteps faded behind her, and she swiped at the wetness on her cheeks. Why did her body betray her like that? Crying did no good.

Rolande's cork-soled shoes made little noise on the pavement as she rushed back to her flat. She turned onto the *boulevard* and stopped. A shadowy form huddled on her front step. Who would come visiting at this time of night? A *gendarme?* One of the Occupiers? *Non.* Either of those would stand straight and self-important. She strode forward, and the person moved.

"Rolande? Is that you?"

"Adele?" Rolande stumbled in relief. "What are you doing here?"

"You are the only person I can turn to." Adele's voice choked on sobs.

Wrapping her arm around Adele's shoulder, Rolande fumbled with the key. After a few tries, she managed to unlock the door, and they staggered inside. She closed the door and turned on the light.

"Come into the parlor. We will talk there. Can I make you *le café?*"

"*Non.*"

"It's still steamy outside. Why on earth are you wearing a cloak? You must be roasting." Rolande reached toward Adele who flinched. The hood fell from her head, exposing multiple plum-colored bruises on her face, and a jagged, blood-encrusted laceration on her cheek.

"Adele! What happened? We must get you to the doctor."

Adele shook her head, then winced and swayed on her feet. Her face paled, and she moaned.

Rolande grabbed Adele before she fell and led her to the burgundy-and-gold Louis XIV sofa. She removed the cloak and tossed it on the matching chair. Propping her friend against an oversized pillow, she jumped up and ran to the closet where she retrieved a bedsheet. She returned to the couch and spread the cover over Adele's prone body.

"You are making too much of a fuss." Adele waved her hand in weak protest.

"Don't be absurd. You are my best friend and would do the same for me. I'll be right back." Rolande hurried into the tiny kitchen and soaked a hand towel under the spigot. She wrung out the cloth and returned to the parlor where she laid the cool material on Adele's forehead. "Better?"

A sigh escaped Adele's swollen and cracked lips. "Much. I am sorry to be a burden."

"Stop saying that. You took me in when I first escaped my captors. I owe you my life. Rest. We will speak later."

"No. Now." Adele pushed herself into a sitting position. Her complexion turned ashen.

"You are even whiter than before. Do not tax yourself."

Tears seeped from Adele's eyes. "I don't want to be alone. Please stay."

Rolande lowered herself onto the end of the sofa and lifted Adele's legs onto her lap. She removed her friend's shoes and tucked the blanket around her feet.

The clock on the mantle ticked off the minutes. Needles of pain pricked her back. She'd sat in one position for too long. Stretching her limbs, she wiggled her toes, but her muscles continued to burn.

Adele startled and opened her eyes. "How long have I been sleeping?"

"Not long. I'm sorry to have awakened you."

"I'm ready to tell you what happened, but you must promise not to share my story with anyone or to do anything about the situation."

Rolande searched Adele's face, then nodded. "I promise."

"I was entertaining one of my regulars, an officer of some importance. I despise him, but he pays well, and more importantly, he has a loose tongue. It is a wonder the Allies haven't won the war sooner considering the number of German soldiers who blab. I have lost track of the amount of information that has been exchanged across pillows."

"What do you do with the knowledge?" Rolande's heart sped up. Was Adele part of *la Résistance*, too?

"I pass it along. I don't know how useful it is, but at least I'm doing my part to get the Occupiers out of France."

"Who do you talk to?"

Adele shrugged, then winced and sucked in a loud breath. After a moment, the lines on her face eased. "I must remember not to move so much." Her mouth curved in a tentative smile. "Anyway, I don't know their names. It is better that way. Tonight, I got greedy to find out more. I pressed the *Oberführer*, and he accused me of being a spy. I denied it, but he obviously didn't believe me." She gestured to her injured face. "He began to beat me. I ran, but he caught me at the top of the stairs. We struggled, and he fell down the steps."

"Is he…?"

"Yes, he's dead. His head lay at an unnatural angle, and his eyes stared at me, glassy and nonresponsive. I had to get out of there. My contact and I have a regular check-in time and place. I don't know how to arrange to meet him. Please, you have to help me get away. I cannot return to my flat. They will accuse me of murder, and I will be executed." She lifted terror-filled eyes. "It's true. I probably wouldn't even get a trial, just sent off to one of those German death camps."

"What can I do?"

Adele cocked her head, a grimace flitting across her face. "You can arrange for a fake passport and false traveling papers. The women in this city call you a *collaborateur*, but you are not. Surely, someone in your network can set me up and get me out of Paris. Please. Help me."

How did Adele know of her connections? Were all prostitutes part of *la Résistance*? Rolande sighed. Oh, that life had turned out differently. She forced a smile. "Of course, I will help you."

Her heart broke into tiny pieces. She was trapped in a life she abhorred and was now going to lose her only friend.

Chapter Four

Simon stood at the edge of camp and gripped the metal cup with both hands to let the coffee's heat seep into his palms. Poorly brewed, the beverage scalded his throat on the way down and served to warm him, but the taste was reminiscent of scorched wood. The temperatures would soar later, but at the cusp of dawn, a chill hung over the tents.

Yesterday's drill had killed some of the interminable wait time, and caused excitement among the men who knew battle was imminent. Muted voices blended with the clink of canteens and mess kits as they ate what passed for breakfast. Across the misty meadow, trees and shrubs were barely discernable in the fog. What lay beyond the ghostly figures? Were the Germans rising to eat as if today was another day on the threshold of a possible battle?

The steady clomping footsteps of Eddie sounded behind him. Taking another sip of the vile liquid, Simon grimaced. Mrs. Williams, his family's cook, would be appalled at the army's attempts at feeding the troops. Even the parlor maid could do a better job.

Eddie stopped next to him, hands in his pockets. "There you are, Simon. You were up and out of the tent early. Is everything all right? It's only been three months since you returned to duty after breaking your leg. Is it bothering you?"

"No more than usual on a damp day. The ache will pass." Simon tossed the cold dregs of coffee onto the ground. "My mind is racing. I've lasted five years in this awful war, a veteran of grisly skirmishes, and I know what to expect during the upcoming attack. You do, too. But the division is filled with a high percentage of replacement troops, still green. Will they be able to handle what is required of them?"

"That remains to be seen, but they've been trained and wouldn't be here if they hadn't passed muster."

Simon shrugged. "I'm not so sure about that. The recruitment age goes to age sixty-four. Are we fighting with old men?"

"Hardly. Don't sweat it. The Jerrys are on the run. Hitler's Third Reich is crumbling. It may take another year or so, but we will win this war."

"But will we survive to celebrate the victory?"

"You are in a dark mood this morning, aren't you?" Eddie squeezed his shoulder. "Perhaps we won't see the end of this thing, but we'll be in a better place, won't we? Sure, I want to live to a ripe old age and bounce lots of grandbabies on my knee, but if God decides to take me early—that's His prerogative. You believe as I do. Don't let the drudgery of this conflict weigh you down."

"You're right, as always." Simon blew out a deep breath. "But I'm beginning to believe grandbabies are not in my future. You and Julia have been going steady since secondary school. I can't seem to stay in a relationship longer than three months. That's about how long it takes the young lady to realize that I'm no prize, despite my parent's deep pockets."

"Nonsense. We've talked about this. There is a special lady out there whom God is preparing just for you. You'll know she's the one when you meet her. I guarantee it."

"You think He handpicks spouses for the entire world?" Simon cocked his head. "Isn't that a bit arrogant?"

"I'm not sure He does that for everyone." He jabbed Simon with his elbow. "Just for those who need some extra help."

"I—"

"Lieutenant Harlow. Lieutenant Dryden."

Simon and Eddie turned. Private Cordell trotted toward them stopped and saluted. "Report to Major Fremont immediately, sirs. He says to hightail it."

They returned his salute. "Thanks, Private," Eddie said.

The young man executed a crisp salute and whirled on his heel, striding toward camp and disappearing into the vapor.

"Guess we'll have to finish discussing my love life later, eh, Eddie?"

"Don't think I'll forget." Eddie grinned and jerked his head toward camp. "Wonder what the major has in store for us."

"Something must have come in over the wires for him to be after us at this hour."

They quick-marched through the base and arrived in front of the commander's tent where a pair of sentries guarded the entrance. They snapped to attention and saluted.

"Lieutenants Harlow and Dryden reported as ordered." They returned the salute. "May we go in? Major Fremont is expecting us." Winded, Simon's voice sounded breathless to his ears.

One of the guards ducked his head into the tent. A moment later he withdrew and held the flap aside.

Simon and Eddie entered the rectangular structure and saluted as they stood at attention.

Major Fremont returned the salute. "At ease, men." He lowered himself into the canvas chair behind a small canvas desk. A wireless set rested near his feet, open and ready. "I've got news for you boys. Your requests to join the 102nd Calvary Reconnaissance Squadron have been approved. The transfers come with promotions to captain which are long overdue." He handed them each a document. "Congratulations. You won't be in charge of any men. Needless to say, your first assignment is to help with some reconnaissance, and according to your file you're the best men for the job."

Simon stiffened and risked a glance at Eddie whose eyes widened, and his Adam's apple bobbled as he gulped.

Major Fremont narrowed his eyes. "Harlow, are your French and German as good as your record says?"

"I don't know about my file, but yes, I speak French like a native. My governess was a Parisienne. I've traveled extensively within the country, and I know Paris like the back of my hand. She secured a German native to teach me their language."

"Excellent. How about you Dryden?"

"Very well, sir. I didn't have a governess, but my best friend while I was growing up emigrated from Germany. We used an altered version of the language as a code. My grandmother is from a tiny village in the south of France and taught me French. I've only been to Paris once, but I've memorized the map."

"Have you now? Commendable." Major Fremont's eyebrow rose, and he gestured to the map on his desk. "The plan is to liberate Paris, and everyone knows it, including the Germans. Therefore, we need to proceed with caution and creativity so we can use an element of surprise. That's where you men come in. Your orders are to slip into Paris and scout out the Germans' defenses. We've got some intelligence from the French Resistance, but General Bradley wants to confirm the information. Don't stay long: only a day if you can manage to collect enough information."

"Yes, sir." Simon snapped to attention. "When do we leave?"

The major chuckled. "At ease, son. Anxious to get going, are you?"

Simon grinned. "Absolutely, sir. Time has been weighing heavily despite training and other preparatory activities."

"War isn't all charging the enemy and battle engagement."

"I understand, sir, but do I have to like the waiting?"

Eddie snorted a laugh, and Major Fremont shook his head, a smile tugging at his lips. "You are to get underway as soon as possible. Report to the quartermaster to be outfitted. Your clothing, identity papers, travel authorizations, and the like must be perfect." Major Fremont saluted. "Godspeed, boys."

They returned his salute and slipped out of the tent. Simon exchanged a glance with Eddie, and in wordless consent, they threaded their way through the camp to where the private found them a mere thirty minutes ago.

Simon paced along the tree line. "Finally, a chance to do something, although I must admit to being frightened. You realize if we're caught we could be executed. Or worse, tortured before they kill us."

Eddie nodded. He stuffed his hands into his front pockets and hunched his shoulders. "I'm glad to hear you say you're afraid. I am too, and I'd be worried if you weren't. Those boys who claim they're not are lying. I get nervous before each battle, but this is different. We're on our own."

"The 102nd Cav wouldn't have chosen us if they didn't think we could do it."

"But Major Fremont must be concerned more than usual. I've never heard him ask God's blessing." Eddie raked his fingers through his shaggy hair. "I better get a letter off to Julia. It might be my last. And you should finish that one to your folks."

Simon's heart skittered. What did a man say to his parents on the eve of his possible death?

Chapter Five

With a tired smile, Rolande clicked off the radio and closed her eyes. The number of so-called personal messages prior to de Gaulle's segment on *Radio Londres* made it clear the Allies were using the broadcast to send coded messages to Resistance cells. Would she receive an assignment as a result?

Her heart pounded at the thought. Even the threat of arrest for breaking the law by listening to the Free French program didn't dampen her excitement that liberation was on the horizon.

A quiet knock resonated at her door. Four taps. The sign for victory. Not the usual sound from clients.

Jumping up, she hurried to the foyer. The knocking repeated, and Rolande peeked out the window. The dim light of the thumbnail moon revealed an unfamiliar woman dressed in a stylish hat and cloak standing on the top step.

Rolande turned off the foyer light and cracked the door to peer into the shadowy darkness. "Yes?"

The woman tossed a glance over her shoulder then back at Rolande. "Adele sent me. May I come in?"

"Adele is gone. She could not have sent you." Rolande began to close the door, but the woman shoved her foot against it.

"Please, it is imperative that I speak with you."

"You there! Close that door!" A man's voice called from the inky blackness.

Rolande hesitated for a fraction of a second then widened the opening, and the woman slipped inside. Rolande slammed the door behind her. Would she regret letting the stranger into her home?

"My name is Ines. I have been sent to warn you. An attempt was made on Hitler's life, and he seeks retribution. As we speak hundreds of anti-Nazis are being rounded up. Anyone remotely under suspicion is being arrested. You must join Adele before it is too late."

"How—"

"There is no time for questions. Hurry. I will take you to the rendezvous point. Pack only what you can fit in a small satchel. No one must believe you left."

"I'm not going anywhere, Ines, or whoever you are." Rolande crossed her arms. "You barge into my house, and I'm supposed to believe you know Adele and where she is, and that you are here to whisk me to safety. How do I know this isn't a trap...that you aren't creating a reason for me to be seized?"

Ines blew out a deep breath. *"Je suis désolé.* I'm sorry. Of course you are doubtful. Let me begin again, but I am risking my life to tell you this. I am part of *la Résistance* cell that operates north of the city. Your friend, Adele, was also a member. She was wise to leave because the morning after she came seeking your help, all but two of us were arrested, tortured, and then executed. There is concern that members' names may have been released."

Rolande shuddered. "What does that have to do with me?"

A frown creased Ines's brow. "The Allies are coming, and only God knows if it will be days or weeks, but life in Paris is going to get much worse before it gets better. The Germans know they have limited time to wreak havoc on our beautiful city and her citizens. You can play me for a fool all you want, but I know you are not a *collaborateur* as many believe. I want to see you live to fight another day."

"I appreciate your concern, but I need to remain here. As you say, the Allies are on their way. It is only a matter of time before the Occupiers will be overtaken. I have survived this long. I will stay for the duration."

"You are being irrational, but must make your own decision. I wish you the best. May God keep you in His hands." Ines opened the door and disappeared into the night.

Rolande's heart tugged. Would the Almighty take care of her? She was not one of His children. Perhaps she should be…

The sun was barely up as Rolande finished dressing. Her family might not be willing to see her, but she had to try to convince them to fight the occupation rather than go along with the status quo, even at this late date. Perhaps if they changed their ways, they would not be punished as severely when the liberators arrived.

Her image in the mirror stared back at her, dark smudges under her eyes a result of not sleeping after Ines's visit. Scenarios paraded through her mind during the night, each one more gruesome than the last. When light began to seep around the edge of the curtains, she rose.

With a final glance in the glass, Rolande grabbed her pocketbook, marched down the stairs and out of the house. Her stomach rumbled, protesting her decision to forego breakfast. Perhaps she would find a market if she didn't lose her appetite after the conversation with her family.

Despite the early hour, the temperature already had a stranglehold on the city. She slowed her pace. Arriving disheveled and perspiring would only give her family another reason to criticize her. Traffic was light with only public transport vehicles occasionally rumbling past, dust flying in their wake.

She coughed and pulled a lace handkerchief from her bag. Holding it over her nose and mouth, she trekked the streets until she arrived at her parent's home.

Her parent's century-old limestone mansion flaunted their wealth and prestige. Over ten thousand square meters surrounded by manicured gardens, the house featured six bedrooms, two parlors, and a ballroom. Below ground, a wine cellar stored hundreds of bottles of *Père's* favorite vintage. His position in the Vichy government was the only reason he still possessed his treasured home.

A lone workman raking in one of the gardens ducked his head as she approached. Everyone in the city was skittish, especially those society felt had no value.

Rolande climbed the stairs and rang the bell. Within seconds, the tuxedoed form of *Monsieur* Varin, the family's butler since before she was born, opened the door. His wooden expression did not change at the sight of her even though he had not seen her in over five years.

She stifled the urge to curtsy, instead she clutched her handbag tight to her chest. "Good morning, *Monsieur* Varin, I am here to see *Père.* Is he available?" He would have already risen. Of that she was sure. But would he agree to see her, the one he felt brought shame and scandal to the family name?

Monsieur Varin gestured for her to enter the ornate foyer where portraits of her ancestors judged her from their gilt frames. Shards of light glittered from the crystal chandelier. "One moment, *mademoiselle.*"

Heavy footsteps trod the hallway above their heads, and she turned toward the stairs. Her father's gait was unmistakable. His large form appeared on the landing.

"Hello, *Père.*"

Her father froze, his face a mixture of surprise, disbelief, and anger…and something else she couldn't identify. Regret?

"Rolande." His voice was barely above a whisper.

"I have to see you. There is a matter of great importance we must discuss. I'm sorry to arrive unannounced, but I thought you might not agree to an appointment."

"Do you know what time it is? It is not proper to come calling at this hour."

She nodded. "I'm aware of the impropriety of the situation, but would you rather I came in broad daylight when your rich and famous friends could see me?"

"*Non.*" He descended the stairs. "That will be all, *Monsieur* Varin."

Monsieur Varin dipped his head and exited the foyer on silent feet.

Father approached, his posture stiff and unyielding. "You must be quick about this. I want you out of the house before your mother rises. Understood?"

"Yes."

He gestured toward the east parlor, and she followed him into the elaborate room. Decorated in shades of blue, the salon was used for entertaining members of the public. Her father had chosen not to take her to the drawing room where the family gathered. Tears pooled in her eyes, and she blinked them away.

She lowered herself onto the Empire-era mahogany sofa and tucked her skirt around her legs. Dropping her pocketbook onto the cushion beside her, she cleared her parched throat. Asking for a drink of water was out of the question. Father would not approve of anything that extended her stay.

"*Père*, I've received information on good authority that the Allies are on their way. Reports differ, but they could be here in a matter of weeks or even days."

"Do you think I don't know this, Rolande?" He thrust out his chest. "I hold an important position in the government. I am privy to many things."

"Of course, *Père*. But when the soldiers come…it may not go well with you. You should flee and go into hiding. The victors will say you are a *collaborateur*. I am worried for your safety."

"Bah. I will be fine. I am just doing my job as I am told. Besides, word is that you are also a *collaborateur*. Are you not worried for your own life? Or will you allow the Allies to use you as you have allowed the Germans?"

Her face warmed, but she held his gaze. "Perhaps not everything is as it looks, but who are you to judge me? You bartered me to the highest bidder to gain favors. Ha! That man used me, as you say, and when he tired of me, he passed me to one of his compatriots. You did nothing to help me. I had to escape the situation on my own."

"*Monsieur* Thibault is an upstanding member of the community. I only have your word for what happened. You smeared his name and brought shame to the family."

She leapt to her feet. "How dare you say that? When I tried to come home, you believed some businessman over your own daughter. You did nothing to save me or return me to this family. I had to make my own way, and I had no choice on a profession. No one would hire me. I was starving and homeless."

Her head throbbed, and her pulse raced. Why had she come here? Her parents deserved to be punished.

Love him as I have loved you, My child. The small voice spoke to her heart, and she winced. Apparently, God thought she was one of His children, and He expected her to see her father through His eyes. A difficult commandment. She took a deep breath. "Forgive me, *Père*. I spoke out of turn. Whatever is past is behind us." She swallowed around the lump in her throat. "I love you and only want what's best for you and the family."

His lips trembled for a quick moment, then the mask of indifference settled back over his face. "It is time for you to leave. Do not come here again. Your behaviors bring shame to my name. You are not part of this family, and you never will be."

Chapter Six

The sun blazed high in the sky as Simon approached Paris with Eddie by his side. Intelligence collected from the Resistance member who arrived in camp under cover of darkness indicated that curfew was strictly enforced. He recommended they wait until late morning to slip into the city. Attempting to enter at night was a sure plan to get caught. As a result, Simon and Eddie burned time until Major Fremont had given them the word to begin their journey.

Simon shielded his eyes with his hand. The macadam shimmered, and heat from the asphalt permeated their shoes. He glanced at his clothing, the crisp gray-green jacket of the field uniform cinched around his waist with a belt, and gray trousers stuffed into gleaming boots. His shoulders sported the *Oberleutnant* insignia, the German equivalent to an American lieutenant.

The original plan had been for him and Eddie to dress as Parisian, but with so few young Frenchmen remaining in the city, it made more sense for them to portray German soldiers. He tugged at the belt to ensure the two bullet holes were hidden. Blood no longer stained the material, but the quartermaster claimed there was nothing to be done about the tears in the fabric.

"Stop fiddling, Simon. If we're to pull this off, we need to carry ourselves with the arrogance of the Jerrys."

Simon glared at Eddie and straightened his spine. "Since when are you an expert on military precision."

"I'm not, but if we're to get out of this alive, we need to act the part, not just look it." Eddie clicked the heels of his buffed black boots and squared his shoulders. "Now, where do you think we can find something to eat?"

They passed a limestone building where a Nazi flag snapped and rippled in the breeze, the large black swastika a blemish on the white circle in the center of red wool. Simon gritted his teeth. How many more days before the flag could be ripped from its moorings?

He studied the store fronts as they walked. What would it be like to have your enemy take over your government, your country? America had managed to prevent that from happening to their continent. *Thank You, Lord, for saving America from the Nazi and Japanese scourge.*

A woman scuttled by, her clothing just this side of rags. According to the major, the occupation had been hard on the city with the Germans buying up everything of value. Only the rich and collaborative still dressed as if nothing had changed.

A pair of German officers approached, and Simon squinted to ascertain the men's rank. The graying, lanky man with a drooping mustache was an *Oberstleutnant*, a lieutenant colonel, and his companion, a thirty-something, Aryan-looking man, wore the insignia of a

Hauptmann, a captain. Simon's heart sped up, and he executed a sharp salute. Would he and Eddie get by without conversation or worse, an order to perform some task?

The colonel gave a curt nod, barely acknowledging them, but the younger man narrowed his eyes and seemed to study him with suspicion. Sweat broke out under Simon's arms and trickled down his spine. He resisted the urge to wipe the beads of perspiration dotting his forehead. Would their mission fail before it had barely begun?

Simon schooled his features in what he hoped passed for a mixture of confidence and unconcern. A peek at Eddie said he seemed to be doing the same. They came abreast of the soldiers, and Simon held his breath.

The captain smirked. "*Wie gehts.*"

"*Gut.*" Simon spoke through stiff lips.

"Pay attention!" The senior officer barked at the captain.

The smirk disappeared on the captain's face that reddened to his hairline. "*Jawohl.*" He glared at Simon as they passed, and their footsteps receded.

A loud exhale sounded from Eddie, and Simon clapped him on the back. "That was a close one, yes?"

"Too close. I hope we don't run up against that captain. He didn't seem convinced of our identity."

"I agree. He's a smart one."

A café came into view, its sidewalk tables littered with a dozen German soldiers, laughing and stuffing croissants into their mouths.

Simon widened his eyes. "I'd hoped to start with a smaller group, you know?"

Eddie shrugged. "Better to blend in, I suppose. Especially if that captain comes back this way."

Simon strode forward and threaded his way through the crowd to the café entrance. He yanked open the door, and Eddie followed him inside. A stooped, gray-haired woman stood behind the counter, a look of resignation on her face. Simon's heart tugged. Her homeland was no longer her own which she must resent, yet she had to earn a living, and perhaps the only way to do that was to cater to the Germans. Would anyone be the same after this terrible war?

He removed his visor cap and tucked it under his arm, then smoothed his hair. Smiling at the woman he held up two fingers, then pointed at a platter of croissants. "*Deux, s'il vous plaît.*"

For a moment, the disinterest fell from her face. "*Certainement.*" She opened the glass case, withdrew the treats, and laid them on a small plate. Her shoes whispered on the tile floor as she shuffled to a small table for serviettes.

Simon placed coins on top of the counter with a smile. "*Merci.*"

She cocked her head, and her lips quirked. "*De rien.*"

His smile widened. He picked up the plates while Eddie grabbed the napkins, and then they headed outside. None of the tables were empty, so he scanned the crowd for someone who might provide inside information. Eddie nudged him and jerked his head toward a trio of soldiers who shared a hip flask. Their flushed faces and overly loud laughter deemed them likely candidates.

He reached their table and dragged a chair out with his foot. Dropping onto the seat, he pasted a sloppy grin on his face and donned his cover, the wool, peaked cap with a leather visor. Now to confirm his native grasp of German. "How goes it, men?" He bit into the pastry and nearly moaned in ecstasy. It had been years since any sort of sugary confection had passed his lips.

Eddie joined them, turning the chair and straddling the seat.

The men returned Simon's smile. The elder of the three who couldn't be more than late twenties waved a lazy hand at his compatriots. "Ziegler. Krüger. I am Fischer."

Simon pointed to his chest then jerked his head toward Eddie as he took another bite. "Hofman. Graf." He wiped his mouth with the napkin. "Not my mother's apple strudel, but it will do, *ja*?"

"That's why we supplement with this." Fischer laughed and took a swig from the flask. "These French are nothing like us. They have rolled over like whimpering puppies."

"Not entirely. My division is part of the advance team, and we ran into a problem coming into the city. Some of their Resistance members blew up a portion of railroad tracks outside of Paris." Simon crossed his arms.

"*Ja.* They are a troublesome lot. Cutting phone lines. Setting explosives." Fischer winked. "But not for much longer. The order came down to round up anyone under possible suspicion. We have already arrested three dozen people today. All who claim they are innocent, of course."

"That seems extreme, don't you think?"

"*Nein.* We cannot let them think we are on the run. The Allies are coming, and we will stand strong, but we don't want the French to think they will be freed. If they have hope, they will fight back. We can't have that."

Eddie rubbed his jaw. "Any word on how close the Allies are? Nothing but rumors in our camp."

Fischer leaned close. "I overheard a couple of officers say the Brits and *Amerikaners* could be here within a week or ten days. I hope we're ready for them."

"You don't think we are?"

Ziegler jabbed Fischer, but he waved him away. "We were supposed to get reinforcements a month ago, but no one has arrived yet. In fact, some of the more elite troops have slipped away."

Eddie's eyebrows shot up. "How many of us remain?"

"Some of us believe there are less than twenty thousand German soldiers throughout the city."

Simon popped the last of his croissant into his mouth and chewed slowly. If this man was right, the Allied troops would have no problem liberating Paris. He wiped crumbs from his lips, then folded his napkin and placed it on the table. "What about tanks? I've seen plenty of those."

With a frown, Ziegler shook his head. "Only seventy or eighty panzers have been accounted for. We should have three times that number." His eyes shifted to the ground. "Personally, I don't think we have a chance."

"Shhh!" Krüger hissed and slashed the air with his hand. "Do you want to be arrested for sedition with that morale-shattering declaration? No matter what you think, you mustn't say it."

"You are right, but I am weary of this war." Ziegler grimaced. "I haven't seen my family in four years. My daughter will not recognize me, and my wife may have learned to live without me."

"A long war indeed, but we must remain strong for the *Führer*." Simon squeezed Ziegler's arm.

"Maybe—"

A series of wolf whistles pierced the air behind him, and Simon whirled toward the noise. A group of soldiers waved and called to a statuesque dark-haired woman walking along the sidewalk. Dressed in an emerald-green suit, she carried a sleek leather handbag, and her hair was swept into an elaborate mass of curls. The makeup on her face was flawless, and her shoes though seemingly high-end, had cork heels. Her pink complexion was the only indication she'd heard the men.

Ziegler whistled, and Fischer cuffed him on the back of the head. "Do you want to be shot? That is *Standartenführer* Wagner's woman, Rolande Bisset. She is off-limits."

"She is a prostitute. He does not have exclusive rights to her."
Ziegler rubbed his hands together. "I visited her just last week. A lovely
Stück Kuchen."

Krüger guffawed. "A piece of cake is right."

Simon stared at the woman. Resplendent in her expensive clothing,
she flashed a look of scorn at the soldiers, then her dark-rimmed eyes met
his.

He shifted, and her gaze shot to his abdomen where the belt had
slipped revealing the bullet holes in his uniform. Crossing his legs, he slid
the strap into place with a gulp. Had anyone else seen the damaged fabric?

A smile transformed her face, and her eyes lit up. "Perhaps you
would like to buy me a treat some time?"

Fischer threw his head back and laughed. "It seems our French tart
has a taste for strudel, *ja?*"

"Show some respect, Fischer." Simon frowned. Why had he felt
the need to defend the woman?

"She doesn't deserve it. She is French, and she is a prostitute."

Rolande's face reddened under her makeup. She ducked her head,
but remained in place.

The hair on the back of Simon's neck prickled, and he turned. A
hefty, ginger-haired SS officer glared at him from across the street.
Simon's breath caught. So much for blending into the crowd.

Chapter Seven

Jostled by a pair of German women in the armed forces auxiliaries whose drab uniforms coined the slur "gray mice," Rolande glared at them. Her face flamed, and the warmth had nothing to do with the day's heat. She would never get used to being insulted, despite her realization that being a woman of ill-repute made her unworthy of respect.

Matching holes in the man's uniform couldn't be anything but the result of bullets, yet he seemed unharmed. Perhaps he had recovered. Couldn't the Occupiers afford new uniforms for their soldiers? What did his furtive glance at the officer next to him mean? He seemed guilty or unsure of himself. She'd yet to meet a German officer who exhibited uncertainty.

A chill swept over her. The brief exchange with him was not enough to provide any proof, but something told her that he was not a German soldier. Was it possible the Allies were already in the city? *God, would You tell me if the libérateurs were here?*

She cocked her head and smiled at the man. His eyes and the imperceptible shake of his head seemed to beg her to hold her peace. Not a gambling woman, she'd give a night's wages to bet he was a spy who'd infiltrated the German ranks.

Was the man at his side a partner?

"Get moving, woman. We are too busy for the likes of you." Fischer sneered.

Her lips clamped shut, she nodded and turned away from the men. Resuming her journey, she walked close to the buildings. If she needed to find the soldier again, his unforgettable crystal gray-green eyes and sharp features would allow her to pick him out of a full platoon.

With her heart singing, she moved away from the stone store fronts. Liberation was on the horizon, no matter what Wilhelm had said. *Dear God, let the Allied troops come quickly. Allow the City of Light to shine once more. I don't deserve Your mercy, but I pray You will pour it over Paris, even if I don't survive.*

"Move aside, woman."

A burly SS soldier elbowed his way past, and she held her tongue. It was unwise to talk back to Hitler's black-coated minions, vicious animals who took pleasure in abusing their captives. Ducking her head, she continued to plod along the *boulevard.*

Hunger gnawed at her belly, and she swallowed against the lump in her throat. She should have eaten something before leaving her home, but the urge to prowl the city had been strong. Now that she'd seen the alleged spy, she knew the nudge she felt was Godsent. Was He really going to save her? Is that why He allowed her to see the man? *Please, God. Let it be so.*

Save them.

Rolande stopped short and cast a glance over her shoulder. "Pardon me," she said to a man standing at the intersection.

He glared at her.

"Did you say something to me, sir?"

"I would never speak to a woman of your profession. Leave me alone." The man turned on his heel and marched away.

Who had spoken to her? Continuing along the store fronts, she sighed. Desperate for liberation, she was hearing voices. Mostly shuttered or dark, the windows were hidden from view or streaked with years' worth of grime. A bit like herself.

Save them.

Sweat slicked her palms. Had the years of occupation finally sent her into the abyss of madness? Surely, she was imagining the words in her ear.

A bookstore came into view, and she stopped in front of the shop. Deceptively calm with clear eyes, her image stared back from the glass. *Non.* She was not losing her mind.

The spies are in danger. I have selected you, My daughter, to save them.

Rolande gasped, then clapped a hand over her mouth. *Father, it's You, isn't it? You have accepted me as Your child, and You are telling me to save that man and his friend.* Her heart seemed to leap from her throat, and her mouth went dry. Helping the men would require more than passing on a tidbit of information. It was harboring spies. Enemies of the Third Reich.

If caught, such an act would get her executed.

In the window's reflection, a young woman pushed a rattling baby carriage, her steps measured and slow. Her face was a blur, but her hunched posture betrayed her discouragement and fatigue.

"I will do as You ask, Lord. Not for me, but for the future of France. For that mother and her baby. For all the children." Heart light, she giggled and preened in the window. She must be at her best to convince the young men to accept her offer of hospitality.

With a deft hand, she smoothed her hair and adjusted her hat to a jaunty angle on her elaborate hairstyle, then tugged the silk skirt into place. Her mind calculated her food inventory, and she smiled. Wilhelm's delivery of several select cuts of meat and fresh vegetables yesterday would do nicely to feed the young men.

One final glance in the glass, then she whirled and retraced her steps to the café. *Please let the men still be there.* Rolande shrugged. Surely God would lead her to the spies if she was to aid in their mission.

She slowed her breathing and added a spring to her step. Moments later she arrived at the tiny eatery. Scanning the few customers who sat in the sunshine, she bit her lip. The mystery soldier remained at the table and his broad-shouldered, dark-haired friend sat with him. Their faces were flushed as they hunkered close to each other, voices low. All but one of the other soldiers had vacated the tables.

Why the red faces? Were they in their cups already? It was but ten o'clock in the morning. Would God have her save a pair of drunkards? He had saved her, a prostitute. She would do His bidding.

Displaying her prettiest smile, she sauntered toward the pair. "Good afternoon, *Herren*, I was too quick with my question earlier. It was wrong of me to ask you to purchase something for me. You are guests in our fine city. It is I who should offer my hospitality. Would you like to join me for lunch this afternoon? Say one o'clock? I can make you a delectable meal, fit for kings."

Her soldier looked up, eyebrows raised in surprise. He peeked at his friend, then shook his head, his gray-green eyes dimming with embarrassment. "No, *Fraulein.* But thank you for your kindness. The army feeds us very well."

Hand on her hip, she cocked her head. "Excuse me, *Oberleutnant…*"

"Hofman. And he is *Oberleutnant* Graf."

She dipped her head in acknowledgment. "The military may assuage your hunger, but my meals are beyond anything they can provide for you. I am offering simple, yet delicious home-cooked food, safe from *prying* eyes."

Graf's gaze shot to her face then toward Hofman. He mumbled something she couldn't hear, and Hofman looked up at her. "What do you know of prying eyes?"

Licking her dry lips, she looked down her nose. "Are you going to keep a lady standing?"

"A woman perhaps, but not a lady." His mouth set in a sneer, Graf sat back and crossed one leg over the other.

Hofman laid his hand on Graf's arm. "There will be no more of that talk." He rose and pulled out the empty chair. "Please, join us."

"*Danke.*" Rolande lowered herself onto the seat and laid her hands in her lap. She leaned toward the men. "I am going to put my life in your hands when I say this. I am part of *la Résistance*. You are in danger of being discovered, and it is my duty to facilitate your escape when you are ready." Her lips barely moved as she whispered the words.

Graf sucked in a deep breath and scrambled to his feet. Hofman yanked him back into his chair. "Sit!"

Two pair of eyes bored into hers, commanding her to explain herself.

"I mustn't stay long. A woman of my…like me doesn't loiter for many reasons." She turned toward Hofman. "You know I saw the bullet holes in your jacket, and as good as your German accent is, it is not native. The conspiratorial looks you continue to toss at Graf tell me you are planning something. Perhaps your plan is nothing more than slipping away from your comrades for innocent fun, but the tension emanating from the two of you belie that. Perhaps my logic is faulty, but I believe you stole the uniform, and you are not with the Wehrmacht, which means you are in grave danger. The Germans know the Allies are coming and are on the lookout for scouts and spies. If you don't come to my house, it is only a matter of time before you are caught, and I'm sure I don't have to tell you what the SS would do to you."

A long moment passed without words, the two men staring at her, a mixture of emotions flitting across their faces.

Rolande rose and tucked her pocketbook under her arm. "Fine. If you don't believe me, then take your chances. I will pray for your souls, because you will die."

"Wait." Hofman spoke through thin lips. "I am a man of faith, a follower of Christ. Your reference to prayer, was it for real?"

"Yes. I am a new believer, only coming to Your God recently, but I have heard His voice. What I did not say was that He told me to assist you. I am stunned He would use a woman such as me, but He saved me, so I can do nothing less than obey."

A smile lit Hofman's face, and her heart skittered. Such a handsome man, but more importantly, a Christian, beautiful on the inside.

She returned his smile. "One o'clock?"

"We will be there."

"*Bien.*" With a flick of her wrist, she slid a tiny paper written with her address across the table.

She turned to leave, and movement across the street caught her attention. Wilhelm stood next to a black sedan glowering in her direction. Her breath caught. Had she put the spies in even more danger?

Chapter Eight

Simon used a serviette to blot at the beads of moisture on his upper lip, then balled up the paper and tossed it onto the empty plate. He put on his cover and blew out a deep breath. A little more than an hour before he and Eddie would make their way to Miss Bisset's home.

What prompts a beautiful and seemingly intelligent woman to enter the ranks of prostitution? If he didn't know what she did, he'd have been attracted to her. Flashing cinnamon-colored eyes set wide in a heart-shaped face, topped by shining chocolate-brown hair. Petite and shapely, she wore her silk clothes with grace and aplomb. Did she know how pretty she was? Certainly desperate times called for desperate measures, but to sell one's body to another for pleasure? Is there no other way for her to provide for herself?

In a different time and place he could fall for her.

Eddie jabbed him with a sharp elbow. "Stop daydreaming about our French tart. We need to get the lay of the land."

A frown drew Simon's features tight. "I asked you not to be disrespectful to her."

"Since when does a tar…prostitute deserve respect?"

"Since she is one of God's creatures." Simon sat back in the chair. "While we were in camp you said we can't possibly understand what these people have endured with Hitler's henchmen in residence. What lengths would you go to if your family was starving or freezing to death? Last winter was the worst Europe had seen in many years."

"You've always been a softie, Simon. I saw the way you looked at her. You're attracted to our Miss Bisset."

Simon's face heated, and he wave his hand in dismissal. "I'll not deny she's charming, but I feel nothing special for her."

"Your red face puts a lie to that statement."

With narrowed eyes, Simon watched the activity on the street. Why had he flushed at Eddie's comment? Assuredly a gorgeous woman, Rolande was a means to an end, nothing more. Rolande? He blinked. In the span of minutes he'd gone from calling her Miss Bisset to her using her given name.

He huffed out a breath and shifted in the chair. Sensing someone's attention on him, he surreptitiously studied the pedestrians. Across the street the burly German officer he'd seen while speaking to Rolande scowled in his direction. Simon stiffened. Should he and Eddie leave the area, or would it be better to act as if they didn't notice him?

Eddie raised his glass to his lips, but rather than take a drink, he spoke from behind the vessel. "Don't look now, but one of the German SS soldiers seems unhappy with us."

"I saw him and was trying to decide what to do."

"I say we ignore the guy. The less interaction, the better. I'll make a big play that we're done here, then we'll head in the opposite direction to your young friend. That way, he won't think we're following her."

"Do you think he's annoyed that she talked to us?"

A shrug lifted Eddie's shoulders. "Who knows? Perhaps he'd rather be at home with the wife and kiddos. Perhaps he's simply bushed. Who can sleep in this heat?"

"I think his attention is more than a question of being crabby."

"Then it's time for you and me to disappear." Eddie made a show of draining his drink. He thunked the glass on the table, wiped his mouth with the back of his hand, then pushed back his chair and stood. He clapped Simon on the back and gestured toward the end of the block. "*Los geht's.*"

Simon climbed to his feet.

The soldier at the next table jerked his head toward the hulking officer across the street. "Looks like you two have come under *Standartenführer* Wagner's scrutiny for speaking with his girl. That's never a good thing. Keep your head low, and with any luck he'll forget about the incident."

Eddie tugged at his jacket. "What are the odds of that?"

The man snorted a laugh. "Slim to none considering he's headed this way."

Simon pivoted to face Wagner, snapped a salute, and stood at attention. Eddie mimicked his actions.

Wagner acknowledged the salutes with a sloppy one of his own, then stepped close and inspected them up one side and down the other.

The bullet holes in Simon's uniform seemed to burn his skin. He'd straightened the belt before turning toward the man, but what if he hadn't completely covered the damaged fabric.

Hands clasped behind his back, Wagner stood near enough for Simon to smell the garlic and cheese on his breath. And wine. Was it too early to be drinking, even in France?

"At ease, men." Brimming with greed and stupidity, Wagner's beady eyes were set deep in his pudgy face.

Filled with anything but ease, Simon loosened his stance. He stared straight ahead. *Father, give Eddie and me the right words to say to this man. Please put Your hedge of protection around us and allow the mission to succeed.*

"You boys are unfamiliar to me. Are you stationed in Paris?"

"*Ja,*" Simon said. "We have a couple of hours before we are due on guard duty."

"You seem to be enjoying the fruits the city has to offer. Food, drink…women." Wagner rocked on his heels. "There is much to be had here. Their *Mädchen* are nothing like ours, eh? French girls are elegant, like delicate flowers waiting to be plucked. Wouldn't you agree?" A smug, vulturous smile appeared.

Simon's stomach clenched. He'd met officers like Wagner before. Men who used their positions to satiate their desires, their lusts. Controlling other people with bravado and bullying.

"Answer me!" Spittle formed at the corners of Wagner's mouth reminding Simon of the rabid dog their gamekeeper had put down. The animal had been dangerous and unpredictable, turning on everyone, including his master.

"*Jawohl.*" Simon and Eddie spoke in unison.

"What were you talking about with that *Fraulein*? The one in the blue suit. She spent a long time with you."

"We are on leave, and she was suggesting activities we might enjoy."

"What sorts of activities?"

Simon pinned what he hoped was a look of disdain on his face. "The Arc de Triomphe, the Pantheon, and the Pont Alexandre III, all of which she seemed quite proud of. Nothing like the Brandenburg Gate or Cologne Cathedral, of course, but acceptable sites, I assume."

"Quite right. German architecture is superior to anything else in the world. Have you been to Neuschwanstein Castle?"

"No, but I understand the views are magnificent. Ludwig II built it in honor of the composer, Wagner. Are you related?"

Puffing out his chest, Wagner shook his head. "*Nein.* But we share a name. His first name was Wilhelm also."

"You must be proud." Simon clenched his hands. Would this conversation never cease?

"*Ja.* But all Germans are proud, are we not? We are the master race."

Simon swallowed the bile that rose in his throat, then forced a smile. "Permission to be dismissed, sir? Our leave expires at eight o'clock tonight."

"Certainly. Have fun and stay out of trouble." Wagner's face turned to stone. "And stay away from the S*trudel* in the blue suit. She is my special friend. I will find out if you disobey me. *Verstehen?*"

Heart slamming beneath his uniform, Simon saluted. "*Jawohl.*" Would seeing Rolande put her at risk? Had she lied about being a member of the Resistance? Was she setting them up with the SS now that she guessed they were spies? Should he and Eddie leave the city without going to her home? Were her claims of faith genuine or a ruse? Too many questions.

After a long stare, Wagner lumbered away. Simon yanked on Eddie's arm, and they hurried down the street. When they rounded the corner at the next intersection, Simon stopped and pulled out his handkerchief to wipe his face. "He didn't ask to see our leave papers."

Eddie rubbed his jaw. "I hoped we weren't going to have to test their accuracy."

"SOE provides the best forgeries in the world. Besides, I don't think Wagner climbed the military ranks through his intelligence. Do you think he would have recognized a fake?"

"Perhaps not, but I'm thankful we didn't have to take any chances." Eddie cocked his head. "Are will still going to Miss Bisset's house?"

"We must. She has crucial information the major will want."

"How can you be sure?"

Simon sighed. "By the nature of her…ah…employment, she has access to the loose tongues of braggarts and drunkards. Just as important, she is our safe avenue out of the city." He met Eddie's eyes. "Obtaining the intelligence is one thing. Getting out with our skin intact in order to deliver it, is something else."

Chapter Nine

The scorching midday sun beat down on the pedestrians who trudged past on the sidewalk outside Rolande's apartment. Eyes downcast, the civilians dressed in dark, threadbare clothes pointedly avoided looking at the German soldiers who strode through the crowd. Dirt and debris littered the streets that prior to the war were pristine. Window boxes on the homes across the street were void of flowers. No one seemed interested in celebrating summer after four years of Occupation.

A young woman, her head covered with a handkerchief, pushed a decrepit carariage. Did she only carry a baby, or was she a Resistance member hiding clandestine documents underneath her child as Adele had done several weeks ago?

Rolande stood in front of the open window in an effort to gain some relief from the stifling heat of her rooms, but no breeze wafted the gauzy white curtains. She'd removed her silk jacket, but her sleeveless silk blouse stuck to her back like a fly on flypaper.

She searched the street below for the British spies. The only uniforms remaining were on a group of SS soldiers leering at a woman on a bicycle. The mantle clock chimed, and her gaze flew to the door. Would the men come as promised? Her breath hitched, and she bowed her head.

Dear God, I am new to being Your child, and I still have trouble believing You would save me, but the one who calls himself Hofman seems adamant that You would do so. Please keep him and his friend safe, and help me spirit them out from under Wilhelm's watchful eye.

Had inviting them to her home been a poor idea? She'd thought if they appeared to be customers, their presence wouldn't be suspicious.

A knock sounded. Rolande's heart skittered. In an effort to relax, she smoothed her skirt and patted her hair. She walked to the mirror that hung near the entrance to check her reflection. Worry lines marred her forehead, and fear radiated from her eyes. "Pull yourself together, Rolande. You must convey a confidence you do not feel or the men will not trust you." She gave herself a curt nod, then took a deep breath and straightened her spine.

With a tug, she opened the door. Hofman and Graf stood in the doorway, hats under their arms. She gestured toward the living room. "Welcome to my home, *Herren.* Please come in."

They entered the house, and she peeked outside. No one hovering on the sidewalk. She sighed and closed the door.

The men's gazes ricocheted around their surroundings, and she looked at her sitting room with new eyes. A gilt-framed Degas hung over the tile fireplace, and a pair of paintings by Mary Cassatt graced the beige wall above the mahogany Louis XIV desk. An ornately carved art nouveau green sofa and matching chairs clustered together on a Persian rug.

Sculptures and figurines lined the shelves of an art nouveau display cabinet.

What did they think of her living quarters? Unable to afford something this grand, she was eternally grateful to Adele's friend for allowing her to live here.

Muffled footsteps sounded in the hallway, and a chill swept over her. The men froze, faces grim. The treads passed her door and faded. She cleared her throat. "We have little time. Please, sit, and I will tell you what I know."

Hofman and Graf exchanged a glance, then lowered themselves on the couch. Hofman leaned forward, an earnest look on his face. "Yes, time is of the essence, but first we must have assurances about your identity and the validity of your information. We took a great risk coming here, and it may all be for nothing, or worse, a ruse to have us captured."

Rolande nodded. "I understand and will try to be as brief as possible." She wiped her damp palms on her skirt then folded her hands. "You already know my name, and I assure you it is real. My father is Maurice Bisset, and he holds a position of importance in the Vichy government. He rose to power by gaining favors among the rich and powerful. He also made it his business to know things about people…things they wouldn't want made public." She hesitated. "How do you say it…the bones in the closet?"

Hofman grinned. "Skeletons. He knows where the skeletons are hidden."

"*Oui.* Anyway, before the war, when I was a young woman, a friend of his wanted someone to accompany him to events. To look pretty and be attentive to other well-placed men. I didn't want to do it, but in France children, especially girls, do what their fathers' demand. I believe *Père* thought this would be a way to gain more power. He filled my armoire with expensive, beautiful outfits, and I attended banquets, soirees, and tea parties. This went on for weeks, and it was not so bad. The man treated me with cold professionalism, and that's how I met my friend, Adele." Adele's face rushed to Rolande's mind, and tears gathered in her eyes. She sniffled and blinked away the moisture.

"Thinking of your friend makes you sad. Did she die?" Simon's forehead wrinkled.

"I don't know. She fled Paris two days ago. I can only hope she escaped safely. She is…was…also part of *la Résistance*, and she was involved in an…uh…incident with an SS officer that resulted in his death. Fearing she would be blamed, she left. It is a good thing, too. Others from her circuit were caught."

Graf cleared his throat and gestured to his watch.

"Of course. My apologies. About six months into the arrangement, the man began to make advances to me, first with comments and innuendos, then uh…physically. I rebuffed him, and he stopped for a short while. Then one night, he overindulged at a party and lured me into a guest room at the host's house, forcing himself on me. When it was over, he threatened to ruin my reputation and my family's if I told anyone. Reputation is everything in Paris."

Hofman clenched his fists. "What a despicable swine. Did you go to your father?"

Tears coursed down Rolande's cheeks, and she nodded. "He didn't believe me. *Père* said *Monsieur* LaLaing would never do such a thing, and he was ashamed of me for making those accusations. He told me to continue doing my job, or he would disown me. I realized then that *Père* cared more for his business than his family, so I made plans to leave home.

"Before I could do so, LaLaing took me to what I thought was another man's house for an event, but the building turned out to be a brothel. He left me there, never to return. I was guarded twenty-four hours a day and forced to see clients. I tried to contact my family through letters, but they were returned to me as undeliverable. I was never able to make a phone call." She swiped the wetness from her cheeks. "One night, an SS officer came to visit and bragged about German plans for Paris and beyond. That's when I decided to collect as much information as I could for *la Résistance* while biding my time for the right moment to escape, which I did three years ago. Now, I live here."

Face warm, Rolande raised her gaze to Hofman and Graf. Skepticism colored Graf's face, but Hofman wore a gentle smile. "Thank you for sharing your story. I'm sorry for what happened to you."

"I—"

"What about the SS officer, the one who warned us off?" Graf crossed his arms and glared at her. "Some self-important boor named Wagner. He says you are his special friend. Why should we believe you are part of the Resistance and not an informant for the Nazis?"

"You have only my word." She shrugged. "I act in ways that make him suppose we are close, that I admire him and his success. It is how I get my information. He is a misogynistic oaf who thinks I am a stupid woman only good for meeting his desires. That assumption makes him careless."

"What about your so-called faith in God. You are a believer, yet you are a prostitute." Graf narrowed his eyes. "And Him telling you to help us? I've never heard a voice from God. Why would He talk to you?"

Rolande's heart pounded. Once again, she was judged and found guilty as she should be. She was a fool to think the mighty Creator of the universe would save her. She ducked her head. "You are right. I am not worthy of God's salvation. I don't know why He would choose to speak to me, but He did. Perhaps, there was no one else to do the job."

"In all of Paris? Highly unlikely." Graf frowned.

She leapt to her feet. "Get out. I am trying to help you, and all you've done so far is question my motives and my life. I am not proud of being a prostitute, but it has been the only way to put food on my table." Her lower lip trembled. "I wish to start fresh, but I must figure out how to make that happen. I have to learn to rely on my Savior, but I don't know how."

Hofman held up his hands as if in surrender. "I'm sorry for Graf's questions, but we can't simply trust your assertions of being in the Resistance and that God sent you." He looked at the other man. "However, I will admit Graf was out of line making comments about your profession. You must give us some intelligence that proves your claim."

"Of course." Rolande rubbed her moist palms on her skirt. "First, as to your comment about reconciling my profession with my newfound faith, God has only recently saved me, and thanks to assisting my clients to overindulge in wine, I've managed to prevent *interaction*. Second, I will give you the most recent intelligence I've gathered." She took a deep breath and shared the facts and figures she'd given to her contact under cover of darkness just a few days ago.

As she spoke, the men's expressions changed from hesitation and disbelief to guarded trust. She finished her recitation and rubbed her eyes.

Simon squeezed her arm. "We—"

Heavy footsteps mingled with the buzz of several voices sounded outside the apartment. The door rattled with a fierce knock. "Rolande, open the door. It's Wilhelm."

Chapter Ten

The knocking on the door continued. *Standartenführer* Wagner called through the door, "Rolande, I know you're in there with the two men we are seeking. It has come to my attention they are imposters, perhaps even spies. *Liebchen,* let me in." The knob rattled. "I was patrolling and saw them come here."

Simon's mouth went dry, and his breathing hitched.

Rolande put her finger to her lips then moved toward the door. "Please give me a moment, Wilhelm. No one is here, but I am not decent."

"You're lying, Rolande." Wagner's words were muffled.

"I know you are anxious to see me, Wilhelm, but you must give a girl the chance to look her best. Believe me, it will be worth the wait." Surprisingly, her voice held notes of teasing and invitation.

Men's laughter rumbled in the hallway.

"That's not why I'm here, and you know it. Open up immediately."

"Not if you are going to be rude." Rolande crept to the desk, picked up a pen, and scribbled on a small piece of paper. She pressed it into Simon's hands and jerked her head toward the stairs in the corner.

He glanced at the note translating the words from French.

GO UPSTAIRS TO ATTIC. ACCESS ROOF. LARGE RUBBISH PILE.

Simon looked into her terror-filled eyes. He stuffed the note into his pocket and leaned close to her ear. "Thank you." Her silky hair brushed his cheek, and his heart thumped wildly. The floral scent of her perfume tickled his nose. He squeezed her hands and crept up the steps, Eddie close on his heels.

———————◆———————

Please, God, don't let me sneeze. Dust and the stench of something dead assailed Simon's nostrils as he laid under the pile of rubble and refuse on the flat roof of Rolande's house. Did he imagine the sound of scampering feet? The brawny rats he periodically caught sight of seemed better off than Paris's human inhabitants. He didn't want a face-off with one of the oversized rodents while trying to maintain his hiding place.

Minutes crawled past. What was going on downstairs? Was Rolande discussing the best way for Wagner to ambush Eddie and him? Surely, she was telling the truth when she said she'd help them escape. *God, You would have given me a sign if this was a trick, wouldn't You?*

Rustling to Simon's right shifted the accumulation of debris. His skin itched in multiple places from the ill-fitting, wool uniform, and sweat pooled under his arms. How long before it would be safe to leave?

The door to the roof opened with a bang.

Simon flinched, then held his breath. *Father, don't let them find us.*

Hobnailed boots tromped across the slate roof, and several voices argued in German.

"As stupid as the *Amerikaners* are, would they hide on top of a building with no way out?"

"Who knows? Just do what you're told and look around."

"What does Wagner see in that woman? He loses all reason in her company. She's pretty enough, but probably not much going on upstairs, I would imagine."

"He doesn't visit her for stimulating conversation—"

"Hey! Over here."

The footsteps thundered away from Simon's location, and he tried to peek through the refuse. Nothing.

Wood hit the surface with a hollow thud, then the noise of stones being moved. Simon closed his eyes and willed his heart to stop slamming against his chest. What were they doing?

"Well, look here." The men guffawed, and the clink of glass filled the air.

"How many bottles did you find?"

"Are they any good?"

"Maybe this will cool Wagner's head about not finding the spies. Let's go. There's nothing else up here."

The men clomped their way to the door. The footsteps faded, and Simon blew out a deep breath. "Eddie, are you okay?"

"Yes, but I'll be glad when we're back in camp."

"Amen to that." *Thank You, Father. We're not out of the woods yet, but it seems You plan to get us out of here safely.*

After what felt like hours, but in reality was probably only minutes, the door opened again. "They're gone for now. You may come out." Roland spoke softly.

Simon coughed and pushed away the rubbish. Sitting up, he brushed off the dust and grime from his clothing. He ran his hands through his hair. Dust rained into his lap. Glancing at Eddie, he grinned. "Do I look as awful as you do?"

Rolande frowned. "Wilhelm did not seem to believe me when I told him that you had already left the city. Follow me."

Simon and Eddie climbed to their feet and finished cleaning their uniforms and boots to prevent making tracks through the house. On soundless feet, they descended the stairs behind her. In the parlor, she handed them a bundle of raggedy clothes she'd secured from her neighbor, *Mme* Perreault, the only one who did not treat her with contempt, then pushed them toward the bedroom. "Change quickly. I will apply makeup to alter your appearance. You will be an old man and woman."

"But—"

"There is no time to argue. You must be gone. Wilhelm will return. That much is certain."

They rushed into the bedroom, and Simon froze. Cobalt-blue silk sheets covered the bed. Blue velvet curtains graced the windows. Artwork similar to that in the parlor hung on the toile-papered walls. A satin robe was draped across a light blue fainting couch. His heart fell. This was where—

"Ouch!" Simon rubbed his shoulder where Eddie had punched it.

"Stop moping over the room and get dressed."

"I wasn't moping."

"Yeah, whatever you say."

With fingers stiff from being unmoving for so long, Simon shed his uniform and donned the faded dress and torn sweater. Too bad it wasn't winter. A heavy coat would go a long way in covering his masculine build.

"I think this is for you." Eddie handed him a small pillow. "Stuff it under the dress, then tie the sash around it. Scuff up your boots. Hopefully, they'll think you stole them off some poor dead soul."

Eddie wore a newsboy hat pulled low over his face. A stained shirt hung over shabby, threadbare pants tucked into a pair of work boots. He beckoned for Simon to follow him before heading out of the room.

Simon's gaze swept the lavish room once more before he hurried to the parlor.

Rolande removed the cap to powder Eddie's hair until it was almost completely white, then rubbed color on his cheeks to simulate dirt. A few deft strokes from some sort of pencil aged his face. She stepped back and studied him for a moment, then waved him out of the chair.

She turned to Simon. "Now, you."

He sat in the chair Eddie vacated.

"Close your eyes, *s'il vous plaît*."

Complying, he sucked in a breath when a stray lock of Rolande's hair grazed his cheek. His face warmed, and he heard Eddie chuckle. Sweat broke out on his palms. What was wrong with him? He was responding to her nearness like a fourteen-year-old school-boy.

Her hands trembled as they rubbed makeup onto his skin. Did she feel the electricity between them, too?

She stepped away, and the spot where she'd stood grew cold. He opened his eyes and found her gaze riveted on his face, her expression a mixture of longing and regret.

A moment passed while they stared at each other, then Eddie cleared his throat. "As fascinating as it is to watch the two of you ogle each other, we must get a move on. What is the plan?"

Rolande blinked and turned away. She ducked her head, then busied herself with stuffing cosmetics into a small beaded bag.

Simon rose and cuffed Eddie on the back of his head. "Don't embarrass the lady."

Eddie grinned and shrugged. "Then stop acting like a lovesick calf." He sobered his expression before he turned to Rolande. "My apologies, miss, no insult intended. I appreciate everything you are doing for us."

"It's nothing." She waved her hand in dismissal and picked up a bag filled with tattered clothing. Thrusting the package into Simon's arms, she said, "Carry this with you, so you seem to have some purpose. I have arranged for you to meet an elderly couple who are leaving the city to visit their daughter in Marly le Roi. It is west of Paris, but it is better that you not be seen headed north, *n'est-ce pas?* Wilhelm or his men are probably still watching the house. You must slip out through the alley."

Simon shifted the bag to one hand, then squeezed her shoulder with the other. "Words are inadequate to express our gratitude. You are doing this at great peril to yourself."

Her cheeks pinked, and he smiled. She was beautiful. On the inside, too. "I wish there was something I could do for you in return."

A guarded look came into her eyes, and she nibbled her lower lip.

"What? We want to repay your kindness."

"It is a lot to ask, but can you save me and my family during the liberation? There will be much bloodshed, and people will be taken captive. Can you promise us safety?"

Simon glanced at Eddie who frowned.

Save her, My son.

"Yes, as God is my witness, you and your family will be protected. However, they must all be here, in your home, when we come. I cannot tell you when that will be, but you must be ready." He cast a glance around the room, then strode to her red silk shawl. "Tie this to your balcony railing. Once the battle has begun, lock the doors and no one must leave. Understood?"

"Oui. Thank you *Oberleutnant* Hofman."

He grasped her cold fingers in his own. "Simon. My name is Simon."

"Simon."

His name on her lips sent his heart skittering. He had it bad. What was he thinking?

Chapter Eleven

Gunfire crackled.

Rolande ducked behind a pile of sandbags. The uprising had started. She shouldn't be outside, but she was desperate to convince her family to understand the end was near, and their safety depended on Simon.

Simon.

What had she done to deserve his help...his care? Her heart swelled. He had feelings for her that seemed genuine. His eyes softened when he looked at her. He treated her with respect despite her profession and demanded others do the same. His touch on her arm or shoulder was gentle, not predatory or possessive.

Shaking her head, Rolande frowned. Who was she kidding? He was only being kind. Someone of his caliber could never love her. She sighed. But it was nice to feel special, even if only for a little while.

She peeked past the armed insurgents over the barricade. The streets were vacant of German soldiers, so the rebels had nothing to shoot. All was quiet for the moment, so she hurried along the sidewalk. At the next intersection she turned right and broke into a trot, the soles of her ballet-style flats slapping on the pavement.

Faded artillery sounded from her neighborhood. The Germans had been retreating east for two days, their tanks and vehicles rumbling down the Champs Élysées. The French Forces of the Interior, or FFI as everyone referred to them, had put up posters on the walls of every building in Paris calling citizens to arms and touting victory was near. She hoped so.

But how many more lives would be lost before the Allies triumphed over the Occupiers?

Ahead of her, a group of men dug trenches in the pavement. Two women approached pushing wooden carts filled with rubble. They sneered at her before looking away. As they passed, one of them hissed, *"Collaborateur."*

Rolande's face warmed, but she drew herself to her full height. *"Non!* I am not." They wouldn't believe her, but she was tired of the mistaken assumption she was a Nazi sympathizer. She could never follow their evil tenets.

Feet aching, she finally arrived at her parents' home. Her heart was in her throat, and her palms were slicked with moisture. Would her journey be for nothing? Would *Maman* and *Père* refuse to see her?

She tucked her handbag under her arm and trudged up the front steps. Her reflection in the glass on the front door revealed her disheveled appearance. She removed her hat and patted her loose chignon back into place, before smoothing her suit. Nothing could be done about the worry lines on her forehead, but perhaps they would serve to demonstrate the seriousness of the situation.

Before she could knock, the door swung open. *Monsieur* Varin stood ramrod straight, his hand on the knob.

"I'm here to see *Père*. Would you please let me in?"

"Of course, *mademoiselle*. Follow me."

Their footsteps echoed on the tile floor as he led her to the parlor. He gestured to the sofa, and dipped his head, a tiny smile on his lips. "It is good to see you again, M*ademoiselle* Rolande. I am glad you are safe."

Tears gathered in her eyes. "Thank you, *monsieur.* I hope my father feels the same."

He exited the room, closing the door with a discreet click. Silence descended. Jittery, Rolande was unable to remain seated. She prowled the room, her gaze bouncing from artwork to sculptures. Any other time, she would revel in their beauty and *Père's* good taste. She rubbed her hands together, chilled even though the room was an oven.

The door opened, and she turned. Henri and *Père* entered and stood shoulder to shoulder, their faces identical, unreadable masks.

She smiled and rushed toward them. "Father, Henri, thank you for seeing me. You won't regret it."

Henri crossed his arm, and a frown darkened his face. "We'll see about that. *Père* is stunned you are here after your last conversation. We want to know why you would come back after he ordered you never to return."

Rolande's eyes widened at Henri's use of French. Maybe he was not as brainwashed by the Nazi's as he seemed. "I'm so glad to see you here safe. Is *Maman* here also? And Louise?"

"*Oui.* They are here as well as the children. We arrived shortly after the fighting began. Our parents' house is off the beaten path. I am hopeful it will escape the rebel's notice." Henri continued to look mulish. "Now, why have you come?"

Her lower lip trembled. "Will you allow me to sit?"

Père blinked as if coming out of a trance. "Of course." He gestured to one of the vacant chairs, then lowered himself onto the sofa. Henri remained standing.

She rubbed her brow. "Henri, please. I don't understand why you are so adversarial to me inside the house. No one can see us talking. Your precious reputation is intact."

"You may have been seen entering."

A sigh escaped, and she shook her head. "Perhaps, but the boulevard was deserted. Anyone not involved in the uprising is staying behind closed doors." She clenched her hands together in her lap and took a deep breath. Arguing with Henri would only make matters worse.

"You didn't remain inside." *Père's* face paled. "Are you involved?"

"Not directly, but I have been part of *la Résistance*. I have used my…er…position to obtain information from the Nazis in order to pass it along to the Allies."

Henri gasped. His mouth worked, but no words emerged.

She rose and began to pace. "For most people, it has been difficult to live under the Occupiers. Their grasping, greedy hands take the best and sometimes the only portions of what commodities are available. The laws and rules serve to squash us under their heels. They want to wipe out any sense of being French, to say nothing of what they have done to the Jews and others they despise. I could not stand by and do nothing."

"Do you think you are better than us who chose to go along, rather than risk our lives by going against them? You are nothing. A prostitute who brought shame to our good name." Henri spat out the words.

Rolande bit her lip to keep from crying out. She must ignore their hatred and persuade them to join her.

"You have no response? You know I am right."

She swallowed against the lump that had formed in her throat. "You are right, yet you are wrong. Yes, I have been a prostitute, and I am sorry you feel the family name has been besmirched because of that. But Jesus has saved me from my transgressions, making me a child of the almighty God. I am a new person, someone of value, now. I am setting aside my profession for Him. I don't know what He has in store for me, but He will provide. Once the city has been liberated, and you know it will be, I am leaving. I will start over wherever He leads me." Her words came out in a rush.

Henri snorted a harsh laugh. "Just like that you are fresh and clean. What makes you think God would save the likes of you?"

"All those years in church when we were children, and you learned nothing, Henri? None of us is worth saving, but He loves us so much, He chose to send His Son."

His face reddened. "And since when are you versed in theology?"

She walked to him and stared deep into his eyes. "We don't have a lot of time. The fighting is only going to escalate and the danger increase. Do you really want to continue sparring with me rather than discover why I have exposed myself to danger to come here?"

Père cleared his throat from behind Henri. "Rolande is correct. The end is near, Henri. We must listen to your sister." His eyes glistened with tears. "I have not done right by her, yet she is here." He smiled at her. "Please, daughter, tell us what we need to know."

Rolande gulped. *Père* had essentially apologized for all that had occurred, and he was looking at her with love. Who was this man? What had happened since he threw her out from this very house just days ago?

Henri dropped onto the sofa next to *Père*. "Fine. Talk."

Thumbing away the tears that continued to stream down her face, Rolande sent a prayer heavenward. *Father, please help me impress upon them the need to come with me.* She sniffled and leaned forward. "Two Allied soldiers came into the city disguised as German officers. Their identities were discovered, and I hid them, then helped them escape. In exchange, they agreed to provide safety for me and my family, but you must come to stay with me. There is a signal that will tell them my house is to be spared."

Eyes narrowed, Henri pursed his lips. "And what is that signal?"

She shook her head. "*Non.* I will not say. If you want to be safe and alive when this is all over, you will get your children and come with me immediately. You cannot carry a valise or anything that makes it appear you are traveling. Bring a jacket if you must, but nothing else. My instructions were clear."

"You have a peace radiating from you, daughter. I can see that you have indeed changed." *Père* rose. "I will advise your mother, and we will come." He kissed her forehead. "Thank you for loving us and…" His voice broke. "And forgiving us."

"*Père —*"

"You can do what you wish, Henri, but it is my hope that you will join us." He turned to Rolande. "We will be ready in twenty minutes."

Shouts came from outside. She grimaced. "Better make it ten."

Chapter Twelve

Predawn fog blanketed the camp as Simon packed his gear in preparation for battle. The order had been given. He and the other American reconnaissance and engineer troops would join Major General Leclerc's French division which led the northern column. Four battalions of the V Corps' artillery would bring up the rear.

His pulse raced as he wiped sleep from his eyes. Rest had not come easy last night knowing fighting was imminent, so he'd written his folks. Unable to share anything of a military nature, he regaled them with sanitized versions of stories about his men. Mom would enjoy the anecdotes, and Dad would read between the lines, having served during The Great War.

Patting the missive in his breast pocket, he smiled. He'd finished the correspondence by emphasizing he thought of them often and felt their prayers. Even now, peace wrapped around him like one of Mom's crocheted blankets. That wasn't to say he'd survive, but he wasn't afraid.

Simon glanced at Eddie who also busied himself pulling together his kit. A muscle in his jaw jumped, his breathing ragged.

"You all right, Eddie?"

Eddie continued to pack.

"Eddie?" Simon leaned over and poked his friend.

"Huh? What?" Eddie's gaze shot toward Simon. "Sorry. Were you talking to me?"

"Checking to see how you're doing. We're seasoned officers, but the adrenaline still pumps before the games begin. You seem more than a bit rattled."

"Just a lot on my mind."

"Want to talk about it?" Simon glanced at his wristwatch. "There's time before we have to fall in."

With a look over his shoulder at the other men, Eddie blew out a loud breath. "You always could see through me, but I'm not sure now is the right time to having a counseling session. The walls have ears, you know."

"We've eaten, slept, and fought together for nearly four years. There's nothing these guys haven't heard." Simon crossed his arms. "Spill it."

"Okay. I didn't do as you suggested and write to my parents. Now, there's no time. Like you said, I should repair my relationship with them. We may not see eye to eye, but we're blood. They love me, and all I've ever done is disappoint them." Eddie looked at Simon, his face clouded with regret. "What if I don't make it today, and I never get to apologize to them or tell them I love them?"

"They'll still know how you feel." Simon understood the heavy burden of guilt. "Back in high school, I lied to my dad about smoking in the garage. I claimed I hadn't, but it came out later that a neighbor had seen me and snitched to my folks. I felt like a heel and was sure they didn't love me anymore for what I had done. Dad isn't the most demonstrative man, but he sat me down and said that no matter whatever I did, including turning my back on him and Mom, they would still love me. So, you can rest assured your parents know your heart."

Eddie fiddled with the strap on his pack. "You think?"

"I know." Simon clapped him on the back. "But let's pray God keeps you safe, so you can write that letter." He scooted closer to Eddie and bowed his head. "Dear Father, thank You for Eddie's friendship. We've been together through thick and thin, good times and bad. You know how he's feeling. Please give him peace about today's fighting. Keep him safe, so he can communicate with his folks. I'd appreciate it if you'd keep me safe too…and Rolande. Convince her family to join her in waiting for us to free them. Please protect them in Your loving arms. In Jesus' name. Amen."

With a knuckle, Eddie rubbed his eyes, then grinned. He thumped his chest. "Your prayers are strong, buddy. It's unexplainable, but the tension is gone. No matter what happens today, I'm okay with it."

"Praise the Lord! You—"

A bugle sounded assembly, and a voice called through the mist. "Fall in!"

Simon jumped to his feet and lifted his pack onto his shoulders. "I guess we're finished here." He followed Eddie toward the troops congregating at the center of the camp.

Conversation buzzed, mingling with the clatter of equipment and thundering feet of hundreds of soldiers. Engines roared to life, and gasoline fumes permeated the air. Murky sunlight pierced the mist.

Strident notes from the bugle quieted the troops and alerted them to stand at attention. Simon congregated with the other officers of the Reconnaissance Squadron and straightened his spine as he watched the soldiers line up. From under the brim of his cover he could see movement as Major Fremont climbed into the back of a jeep and stood.

"Men, we've come a long way from Normandy. We're in the last stretch of this conflict, but it's not going to be an easy victory. Our enemy has fought hard against us. Intelligence tell us there are twenty to thirty thousand German troops in Paris. Many seem ready to lay down their weapons, but just as many will not give up. Be prepared for snipers once we enter Paris. Be vigilant about civilians. Those not part of the French Forces of the Interior have been cautioned to remain inside, but we cannot be sure they will do as instructed. Godspeed and move out!"

The ground vibrated underneath Simon as men and equipment behind him rumbled toward Paris. Sweat trickled between Simon's shoulder blades and formed on his hairline and upper lip. Another scorching, dusty day in France.

Miles passed as the sun rose. His feet throbbed, and he licked his dry lips. Unscrewing his canteen lid, he took a deep swig. Warm liquid trickled down his parched throat. Once inside the city, he and the other Squadron members would break away for their own mission.

Ping!

A bullet grazed the canteen and shot it out of his hand. He grabbed his Browning and swung it in the direction of the shooter. A hail of fire came from among the trees to his left, and he led a unit into the forest on the other side of the road while other men took cover behind the jeeps and trucks. Tanks swung their guns toward the enemy, firing at will. Smoke curled above the combatants and infiltrated the foliage.

Simon coughed and squinted to get a better view. Across the expanse, a German soldier crept past a large rock. Simon closed one eye and peered down the gun sight aiming the crosshairs. He pressed the rifle butt against his shoulder and squeezed the trigger. An explosive boom reverberated in his ears, and the man dropped behind the boulder.

Swallowing against the lump forming in his throat, Simon shook his head. He would never get used to taking another man's life. *Please, God, comfort his family.*

The combat continued for about thirty minutes, then silence descended from the German line. The command came to fall back into formation, and Simon jogged to the road. His head swiveled to find Eddie. He craned his neck to see around the swirling mass of soldiers, his gaze seeking the lanky frame of his friend.

A pair of arms lifted amid the crowd, and Eddie's distinctive whistle split through the confusion. "Simon, over here!"

Simon shoved his way through the chaos. He grabbed Eddie in a bear hug and pounded him on the back. "You made it through. Are you injured?"

"Nah. Not a scratch. Jerry's aim is terrible." Eddie guffawed, his teeth white against the grime on his face. "You?"

"Nothing. I'm okay." Simon sobered up. "I saw Ron and Charlie go down. I don't know if they bought it or not."

"They're good guys. Hopefully, they'll make it."

"I pray you're right." He slung his rifle onto his shoulder as they resumed the march toward Paris.

High in the sky, the sun followed them as the day progressed. Twice more they were caught in skirmishes, and twice more the Allies squelched the attacks. By evening the column was still about five miles from the closest entrance to Paris when civilians swarmed the troops, engulfing them with cheers, kisses, flowers, and wine.

Simon extricated himself from the particularly ardent embrace of a grateful French woman. Some of his compatriots didn't seem as eager to disengage themselves. So much for French citizens staying inside their homes. Eddie saluted him with a bottle of Burgundy and a smirk.

Movement toward Paris stalled as the celebration ebbed and flowed. Simon raised himself on his toes, surveying the activity of

Leclerc's troops. They didn't seem to be in a hurry to liberate their capital city. Why were they procrastinating?

Time passed as Simon continued to reject the advances of women and girls. Reluctant to stray far, he moved out of the swell, close to a nearby stone wall. Minutes later, the bugle called, and someone shouted for the Americans to form their columns. Much groaning accompanied the order, but eventually the men lined up and commenced their march. The civilians melted away.

Two hours later, the troops crossed the Seine behind a detachment of tanks and half-tracks by way of the Pont d'Austerlitz. Following the directive, they spread out among side roads and headed toward the Hôtel de Ville.

Rifle ready, Simon signaled for Eddie to join him, and they crept along an alleyway. House by house they searched for Germans, but found none. His stomach growled. He'd eaten nothing since breakfast. He pushed aside the thought and continued to prowl the streets.

At the next intersection, he hunkered close to the building and peeked around the corner. No human movement. Simon hunched over and trotted along the sidewalk until he came to the intersection. On the wrought-iron balcony above, a scarlet shawl snapped in the hot breeze, and his heart slammed against his ribs. Rolande was waiting for him.

Chapter Thirteen

"Don't stand near the window. Do you want to be killed?" Rolande yanked on Henri's sweater.

He brushed away her arm. His eyes narrowed. "I can't believe I let myself be talked into hiding out in a house—your house—during the uprising. Your notion that some American soldier is going to keep us from harm is foolish, and now we're trapped in here waiting to be executed. We should have left the city when we had the chance. It may not be too late."

"Go ahead and leave, Henri, but once the door closes behind you, we cannot let you back in. The instructions were quite clear."

Louise rose and stepped to her husband. She wrapped her arms around him from behind and leaned her head on his back. "Please, Henri, do as Rolande says. We must trust her." Her muffled voice quavered. "She would not have had us come here if she thought we would be in danger."

Henri turned and enveloped Louise in a tight embrace, tucking her head under his chin. He stroked her hair and met Rolande's eyes with a troubled gaze. "I was doing what I thought was best for my family, you know. For Louise and the children. I had to provide for them. Your…occupation…it was impacting my ability to do that. I had to choose. Don't you see?"

Rolande swallowed at the lump growing in her throat. "Did it ever occur to you to help me so I wouldn't have to…do what I did? If you had welcomed me into your home instead of believing *Père's* lies that I had chosen my profession…well…things would be different, wouldn't they?"

"Rolande! How can you make such an accusation?" *Maman* jumped up from her seat. "That's not fair to your father."

Père raised his hands in surrender. "Yvonne, please sit. Rolande is correct. I didn't treat her as a father should. She has been left to the devices of men to make her way. I regret that I didn't believe my own flesh and blood when she came to me. I am ashamed." His eyes glistened with tears. "I am thankful she seems to have forgiven me, or at least loves me enough to care whether I live or die."

Rolande's heart squeezed. Had she absolved him of his guilt?

Forgive him, My child, as I have forgiven you.

She gnawed the inside of her cheek. God had cleansed her, the worst of all sinners. Surely, she must do as He commanded. She took a deep breath, then reached out. "Yes, *Père*. I do forgive you."

He hurried across the room and grasped her hands.

Henri snorted. "Suddenly, we are the happy family after all that has happened? Rolande can forget being shunned by us? *Forgive me* for being skeptical."

"I understand your suspicion, Henri, but God has changed me. He is the reason for my attitude. Will I forget? *Non.* Will I no longer feel hurt at the memories of what transpired? *Non.* But I can choose to set aside my anger. I hope you will do the same one day."

Mute, Henri pivoted on his heel and strode to the sofa. He dropped on the cushion and crossed his arms.

"Son—"

"*Non, Père*, perhaps in time. But I will do as you say and await for *les Américains.*"

Louise patted his jiggling leg, and the motion stopped. Leaning his head back on the plump padding, Henri blew out a loud breath. An uneasy silence filled the room.

Hours passed. Shouting, the rumble of vehicles, and periodic gunfire faded to nothing.

Rolande set aside her Bible and climbed to her feet. She gestured to Henri's children. "Oscar, Lilianne, come with me. Let us wash your face and change into clean clothes. We must be ready when they come."

The youngsters scrambled to their feet and skipped across the floor to grasp her hands. The warm grip of their palms on hers brought a smile to her lips. Such was the trust of little ones. As she headed to the bathroom, she glanced over her shoulder at the adults. "It wouldn't hurt you to do the same."

Rolande and the children entered the tiled room, and she set them on the side of the clawfoot tub. She made quick work of scrubbing their faces and washing their hands. Flushed, they grinned at her, and she tapped her index finger on each of their noses. "Don't you feel better?"

She lifted them down, then knelt and encircled them with her arms in a tight hug. Her heart tugged. Henri had forbidden her to interact with Oscar and Lilianne over the years, so she barely knew them, but somehow she loved them.

Four-year-old Oscar looked at her with wonder. "You smell nice, *Tante* Rolande, and you have a very pretty house. Why haven't we played with you before? Can you go outside yet? Will we get to come here again?"

"Uh—" She cringed. How to answer the little boy?

Older by three years, Lilianne jabbed her brother. "Don't ask so many questions, Oscar. Just be happy we are here now." She giggled. "He's right. You do smell good."

Rolande smiled. "So do you."

Lilianne brought her wrist to her nose and sniffed then wrinkled her forehead. "I smell like soap. I want to smell like roses, just like you."

"Come. We must put on fresh clothes."

The children grabbed her hands, and Rolande led them to her bedroom. She opened the satchel Henri had brought against her advice. Rummaging inside, she found a dress for Lilianne and short pants and a shirt for Oscar. "Do you need help, or can you dress yourselves?"

Oscar thumped his chest. "I am a big boy. I can do it myself."

"Silly me." Rolande brushed the hair from his eyes. "Of course you can. I will wait outside." She winked at Lilianne before she stepped out of the room and closed the door.

Dear Father, they are such precious children. Thank You for letting me have this time with them. I don't know what will happen in the future, whether Henri will allow me to see them or not, but I now have a memory I can treasure. She sighed and laid her head against the door. Their muffled high-pitched voices wafted through the wood.

Behind her, loud banging rattled the front door. Her heart leapt into her throat. Was it Simon or Wilhelm?

"Rolande! Come quickly." Her brother's voice held a note of panic.

She opened the door to the bedroom and poked her head inside. "You must stay in here until I come for you. Understand?"

Their eyes wide, Oscar and Lilianne nodded.

"Very good." Rolande closed the door and rushed to the parlor as the knocking continued. Louise and *Maman* clung to each other, faces pale. Henri stood behind the couch, clutching the back as if its cushioned frame could save him. The picture of tranquility, *Père* waited by the door, his hand on the knob. Was he as calm as he looked? No wonder he'd risen to power. Nothing seemed to overwhelm him.

"Rolande? It's me, Simon. The fighting has ceased, and the remaining Germans have been captured. It is safe to come out."

Père looked at her, and she nodded. He yanked open the door. Simon stood on the porch, his face gray with fatigue, his uniform and boots dirt-encrusted. A rust-colored stain covered his right arm and most of his chest.

Her breath hitched. Had he been injured? She rushed forward then stopped in the middle of the parlor. "Simon! Are you hurt?"

He glanced down and shook his head. "No. Eddie…He was hit…I carried him." His dismayed expression worsened as his words tumbled over one another. "It was rough going for a bit, but I was able to get him to an aid station."

"Is he…?"

"The medics are working on him now. They say he's going to make it. The bullet came out of nowhere. We'd been watchful of snipers all day, then we rounded the corner, and I saw your shawl on the balcony. As we crossed the intersection, Eddie was shot from the building opposite yours."

Rolande launched herself into his arms, sobbing. "Thank you for keeping your promise to come for us." Henri had considered leaving and taking his family. The sniper would surely have killed them all. "Thank you, Simon." She continued to weep as his arms held her, strong and secure. He hadn't forgotten her.

———————◆———————

Morning sunlight filtered through the grime on the windowpanes in the opulent parlor at the Hôtel de Ville. Simon sat next to Rolande on a floral sofa, his hands cradling hers. Her family was tucked away in one of the few available rooms upstairs. Leclerc's division had secured the hotel around midnight, and he was now on his way to the Hôtel Meurice to receive Commander von Choltitz's surrender. Rumor had it that General de Gaulle would arrive soon to assume control of the city.

"Rolande—"

"Simon—"

He squeezed her fingers as their words collided. "You first."

She ducked her head and withdrew her hands from his. A slight blush stained her cheeks, and she fidgeted on the cushion. "I appreciate all that you have done for me and my family. It is a lot to ask, but can you help me get to Marseille? The others want to stay in Paris, but I need a fresh start, one where I can be the Rolande of my girlhood. I've always wanted to live near the ocean. Perhaps I can get a job in one of the shops down there. I don't have a lot of skills, but I can learn."

With his finger, he raised her chin until their eyes met. "I'll have to talk to the commander about getting some leave, but would you consider living near my ocean instead of going to Marseille?"

Her eyes widened, and her mouth formed a tiny O. "*Your* ocean?"

Chuckling, he brushed a stray strand of glossy hair away from her face, then stroked her jaw. Her skin trembled under his touch. She must feel the current between them, too. His heart raced. "Please consider what I'm about to say. I may ramble a bit, because my thoughts are jumbled, but hear me out."

She nodded, and he cleared his throat. He hadn't been this nervous since boarding the troop transport in New York City a lifetime ago. "We've only known each other a few days. The hours we've spent together can barely be counted on two hands, but I have seen your gentle spirit, and your love of God that flows over everyone you meet. You care for your family despite all that transpired, seeming to hold them no ill will. And you are more beautiful than any woman I've ever seen." His breath caught. "I'm drawn to you like I've never been to a woman. Until I met you, I was convinced I would never find a special someone with whom I wanted to spend the rest of my life. What I'm trying to say is I'm falling in love with you, Rolande, and I hope you feel the same about me."

Tears welled in her eyes, and she blinked them away. A tremulous frown fluttered on her brow. She rose and walked to the fireplace where she stared at her reflection in the gilt-framed mirror hanging above the mantle. "You cannot possibly love me, Simon. You know what I was. Every young man should have an unsullied girl he can take home to *Maman*. I am not that girl, but you are very kind to say these things."

"Kind? Kindness has nothing to do with this." Simon leapt from the couch and strode to her. He gripped her shoulders. "You are the last thing on my mind before I go to sleep, and the first thing I think of when I awaken. I ache when we're not together, and I wonder what you are doing. During the uprising, I had to think of you as safe and alive, or I wouldn't have been able to cope and perform my mission." He tugged her to him. "Yes, I know what you were. But that is no more terrible than the wrongs I've committed. God views all sins the same, and He cleanses them when we ask Him to. You are a new creature, and your past no longer has a hold on you."

She extricated herself and studied him. A moment slipped by, then a look of wonder bloomed on her face. "You do care, don't you?"

"Yes. Very much. I don't understand how love can happen this quickly, other than to think it is a miracle from God." He leaned toward her, his lips hovering inches above hers. "I will spend every day I have left on this earth thanking Him for it. For you." He lowered his mouth to hers, drinking in her lips' sweetness. They softened and warmed, and she wilted against him.

A sigh escaped her, and he pulled away. "The war can't go on much longer. Please, say you'll do the honor of becoming my wife as soon as possible."

A shy smile lit up her face. "*Oui.* I would like nothing better than to be your wife, Simon." She giggled. "And I will live near your ocean, but perhaps we can visit Marseille on occasion."

The End

What did you think of *Love's Rescue?*

Thank you so much for purchasing *Love's Rescue*. You could have selected any number of books to read, but you chose this book.

I hope it added encouragement and exhortation to your life. If so, it would be nice if you could share this book with your family and friends by posting to Facebook (www.facebook.com) and/or Twitter (www.twitter.com).

If you enjoyed this book and found some benefit in reading it, I'd appreciate it if you could take some time to post a review on Amazon, Goodreads, Kobo, GooglePlay, Apple Books, or other book review site of your choice. Your feedback and support will help me to improve my writing craft for future projects and make this book even better.

Thank you again for your purchase.

Blessings,

Linda Shenton Matchett

Reader's Guide

1. Rolande is falsely accused of being a collaborator with the German occupying forces. Have you ever been falsely accused of something? How did that make you feel? How were you able to resolve the situation?
2. The Germans occupied France from June 1940 through August 1944. Many of the mandates outlawed items inherent to French culture such as wearing a beret or speaking French. How do you think you would have felt (and reacted) to an occupation?
3. Deprivation was widespread in France (and especially the cities where there was little land on which to grow food). People stooped to using the black market, stealing, and other ways to provide for themselves. Rolande was a prostitute. How would you have attempted to provide for you and your family? Would you have considered breaking the law?
4. The French Resistance performed acts of sabotage and other guerilla warfare tactics, provided first-hand intelligence, published underground newspapers, and maintained escape networks for Allied soldiers and airmen trapped behind enemy lines. An estimated 8,000 or more members of the Resistance lost their lives. Would you have been brave enough to participate?
5. There are several secondary characters. Are there any who stand out to you? What was it about them that attracted you to them?
6. Think about ways *Love's Rescue* points to better things to come through Jesus Christ.
7. What lessons from this story can you apply to your own life?

Historical Background

Dear Reader:

    I hope you enjoyed *Love's Rescue*, a modern retelling of the biblical story of Rahab. Please consider reading the original story found in the second chapter of Joshua. Scholars disagree over whether the Old Testament Rahab is the woman listed in Matthew's genealogy of Christ as the wife of Salmon and the mother of Boaz. I would like to believe she is the same woman who couldn't help but fall in love with her "knight in shining armor."

    During my research, I found several parallels between the Israelites' story and the Allies' liberation of Paris in 1944, which enabled me to merge the two stories:

- The folks in Jericho knew the Israelites were coming, as did the Germans about the Allies;
- The exploits of the Israelites were well-known by the inhabitants of Jericho. With the technology available at the time, the Germans (and all combatants for that matter) were aware of the Allied victories leading up to the liberation.
- Memoirs by German soldiers indicate many of them were afraid of how they would be treated by the Allies once they were captured. The residents of Jericho felt the same way (Joshua 2:11 "And as soon as we had heard these things, our hearts did melt, neither did there remain any more courage in any man, because of you…")
- Prostitutes in biblical times were an accepted, yet belittled member of Israelite society. In France, prostitution was legal, with laws mandating what was (and wasn't) acceptable. During WWII, many prostitutes were

considered to be in collaboration with the Germans and treated with contempt by a large portion of the population.

The Liberation of Paris (also known as the Battle for Paris and Belgium) occurred between August 19 and August 25, 1944. Knowing the Allies were on their way, the German occupying forces increased their activities of rounding up suspected Jews, Resistance members, and any other "suspicious" people.

The French Forces of the Interior, known as the FFI, (the armed troops of the French Resistance) plastered posters all over Paris calling citizens to arms. Shortly thereafter, the FFI staged an uprising against the German garrison. Barricades and trenches were constructed as skirmishes peppered the city. On the 22nd, the Germans attacked the Grand Palais, an FFI stronghold and fired upon the barricades. Fighting was fierce and continued off and on for two days until the 2nd French Armored Division and the 9th Armored Company rolled into Paris with tanks and half-tracks. At 3:30 PM on August 25, German General von Choltitz surrendered and taken prisoner. President of the Provisional Government of the French Republic Charles de Gaulle arrived later the same day and moved back into the War Ministry.

Acknowledgments

Although writing a book is a solitary task, it is not a solitary journey. There have been many who have helped and encouraged me along the way.

My parents, Richard and Jean Shenton, who presented me with my first writing tablet and encouraged me to capture my imagination with words. Thanks, Mom and Dad!

Scribes212 – my ACFW online critique group: Valerie Goree, Marcia Lahti, and the late Loretta Boyett (passed on to Glory, but never forgotten). Without your input, my writing would not be nearly as effective.

Eva Marie Everson – my mentor/instructor with Christian Writers' Guild. You took a timid, untrained student and turned her into a writer. Many thanks!

SincNE, and the folks who coordinate the Crimebake Writing Conference. I have attended many writing conferences, but without a doubt, Crimebake is one of the best. The workshops, seminars, panels, critiques, and every tiny aspect are well-executed, professional, and educational.

Special thanks to Hank Phillippi Ryan, Halle Ephron, and Roberta Isleib for your encouragement and spot-on critiques of my work.

Paula Proofreader (https://paulaproofreader.wixsite.com/home): I'm so glad I found you! My work is cleaner because of your eagle eye. Any mistakes are completely mine.

Thanks to my Book Brigade who provide information, encouragement, and support.

A heartfelt thank you to my brothers, Jack Shenton and Douglas Shenton, and my sister, Susan Shenton Greger for being enthusiastic cheerleaders during my writing journey. Your support means more than you'll know.

My husband, Wes, deserves special kudos for understanding my need to write. Thank you for creating my writing room – it's perfect, and I'm thankful for it every day. Thank you for your willingness to accept a house that's a bit cluttered, laundry that's not always done, and meals on the go. I love you.

And finally, to God be the glory. I thank Him for giving me the gift of writing and the inspiration to tell stories that shine the light on His goodness and mercy.

Other Titles by this Author

Romance

Love's Rescue, Wartime Brides, Book 1

Love Found in Sherwood Forest

On the Rails

A Love Not Forgotten (Let Love Spring Collection)

A Doctor in the House (The Hope of Christmas Collection)

Mystery

Under Fire

Murder of Convenience, Women of Courage, Book 1

Non-Fiction

WWII Word Find, Volume 1

Let's Connect!

www.LindaShentonMatchett.com

www.facebook.com/LindaShentonMatchettAuthor

www.twitter.com/lindasmatchett

www.pinterest.com/lindasmatchett

www.linkedin.com/in/authorlindamatchett

https://www.amazon.com/Linda-Shenton-Matchett/e/B01DNB54S0

Sign up for my newsletter and receive a FREE short story

https://bit.ly/2MXJFgC

Interested in more historical fiction?

Visit http://www.lindashentonmatchett.com/p/books.html